HOLLOWED

A Sacred Dark Romance

A.K. ROSE

I was sent to burn.

Wrapped in red silk and oil. Trained to kneel. Offered to a god who never came.

But the fire didn't take me.

He did.

His gaze burns deeper than the fire ever could.

He doesn't speak.

He doesn't kneel.

He doesn't save.

He watches.

He binds.

He anoints.

He ruins.

And somewhere between his silence and my ache, something sacred was born.

What rises from these ashes is no longer woman, but vessel.

Bound to him by vows no church would sanctify.

I wasn't made to be saved.

I was made to be *kept*.

A sacred dark romance.

Chapter One

I KNEW WHAT THE RED SILK MEANT.

I knew before they dipped it in oil, before they brought the basin to the center of the stone floor, before the eldest among them whispered, "Hold still, daughter."

I was not her daughter.

And she did not say it like comfort.

The chamber had no windows. Only a hole in the ceiling, far above, where smoke was meant to rise. Where prayers went to die. Where I looked once, and never again. I sat on my knees, naked but for the modest cloth wrapped around my hips, shoulders bare, back arched from the cold. The stone beneath me was not cruel. It was indifferent. It had held hundreds before me.

It would hold hundreds more.

The silence was not empty. It was heavy with breath, with waiting. I could hear the oil thickening as it warmed over the small flame beside the basin. I could smell the ash already stirred into it. Not incense—this wasn't blessing. This was binding.

I didn't ask why they chose red. I didn't ask why they burned the blue robes we had worn for years. I didn't speak at all. Not because I was obedient. But because I had learned that asking made the hurting worse.

I thought they might hum. Sometimes they did. Low and tuneless. A circle of women pressing sound into our bones so we'd forget what silence was supposed to feel like. But this time, they didn't.

This time, they were quiet.

A hand gripped my chin. Not rough. Not kind. Just firm enough to tilt my head back. Another hand held the oil. Poured it slow, deliberate, over my forehead. It ran down between my brows, along the bridge of my nose, catching on my lips before sliding to my throat.

"For clarity," she said.

It stung. The ash. The heat. The indignity.

But I did not flinch.

Another hand. Across my collarbone.

"For silence."

Oil followed the curve of my neck. Sank into the hollow between my breasts. Crawled like something alive toward my stomach.

A third hand. Pressing low, too low. Palms curved around the bones of my hips, fingers slipping toward the top of my thighs.

"For obedience."

My skin screamed.

But I didn't. I bit down on the inside of my cheek until I tasted blood.

The red silk was brought out last. Drenched. Heavy. Coiled like something dead in the eldest's arms. She began at my ankles, wrapping tight, winding it up my calves, my knees, my thighs. She paused at my hips, looked at me like I wasn't supposed to exist, and then wrapped it higher.

Waist. Ribs. Breasts. Shoulders.

She wrapped me like a corpse.

"Stand," she said.

I did.

The silk clung. The oil made it worse. I felt every breath stretch the fabric. Every inch of me felt touched. Not by hands. By something worse.

Expectation.

I thought maybe, at the end, they would bless me. Speak my name. Give me back some part of myself before they took the rest.

But they didn't.

They turned away. Opened the doors at the far end of the chamber. Let the cold rush in.

And beyond those doors—

I saw it.

The chapel.

Already burning.

They didn't speak when they dragged me from the chamber. My feet slipped on the stone, raw from kneeling, and the moment I hesitated—just once, just one breath too long—a hand gripped the back of my neck.

"*Walk,*" someone hissed. Not in anger. In finality.

I did.

I walked like a body walks to a grave it dug with its own teeth.

The corridor smelled like mildew and smoke. Damp stone giving way to dry rot. Every step I took sent the red silk dragging behind me, sodden with oil, sticking to the insides of my thighs. My skin itched. Burned. My breath tasted of ash and something worse—

Like old blood.

I reached for the walls once. Just to steady myself. The nun behind me struck my wrist hard enough to numb my fingers. Pain flared like something in me broke. I bit down on my tongue until I felt it split.

It was not a procession. It was a disposal.

No chanting. No prayer.

Only the sound of my breath and their footsteps. Me, shuffling like an animal too stunned to bolt. Them, moving like shadows trained to guide the dying.

When we reached the last arch before the chapel doors, they stopped. I didn't.

I turned.

There were four of them.

I knew them all. I had served their tea. Washed their bedding. One had combed my hair when I was ten. Another once held me when I vomited blood during my first fast.

None of them met my eyes.

But *she* did.

She stepped forward from the dark.

The veil she wore was bone-colored. Threadbare at the edges. Her hands were bare. So was her mouth. No silence for her today.

My mother.

She looked at me like I was a dish she'd forgotten in the sun.

Spoiled. Useless. Burdensome.

I tried to speak. My throat convulsed. The words didn't form. Only breath. Only ache.

She raised her hand slowly, like a blessing.

I thought—I was stupid enough to think—that maybe she would touch my cheek. Maybe she would say my name, even if only to let it die between us.

But she pushed me.

Hard.

I stumbled forward, the oil making my feet slip. The doors opened ahead of me with the wind. Smoke rushed out like a mouth inhaling. I choked. My knees hit the threshold.

I looked back.

They stood in perfect formation one moment—a line of shadows witnessing my fate.

Then, like smoke inhaled by stone, they vanished. Not one by one. All at once. As if the corridor itself swallowed them whole.

She was gone. They were *all* gone.

The doors closed.

And I was alone.

Except for the fire.

It reached for me like it knew me. It curled around the altar, licked the stone, tasted the remnants of the girls who had been made holy before me. The heat slapped my face. My vision blurred. The veil began to smolder.

I turned my head, shielding my eyes.

And still I did not move.

I waited for the burn.

I waited for God.

I waited for someone to call me by name.

But all that came was heat.

And behind it—

Something else.

Not voice. Not shadow.

A presence.

Waiting.

The silk went first.

A hiss. A snap. A flare.

It lit at the hem and traveled upward like a verdict. The oil made it fast. Hungry. Ribbons of red twisted into flame, devoured my legs in seconds. I screamed. Not because of the fire.

Because of the sound of it.

Because it sounded like something being born.

The heat hit my skin, then my scalp. The ends of my hair curled and burned, the bitter smell curling up into my throat. I screamed and clawed at the wrap, hands shaking, nails splitting against soaked fabric. I ripped it from my thighs, from my chest, from my arms, until I stood half-naked, covered in oil and smoke and sweat.

Alive.

Not untouched. But not dead.

The fire had kissed my skin—left it red and tender where the oil had burned too fast, raised welts along my arms like brands half-formed. But no char. No blackened flesh. The flames had tasted me and pulled back, as if I wasn't meant for consuming.

My cheeks burned. My lungs seized. I dropped to my knees, coughing into my palm, tasting blood and ash. The fire had not finished the job.

And I was not going to wait for it to change its mind.

I turned to run. Toward the door. Toward stone. Toward anything that didn't want to consume me.

My hands hit solid wall.

Stone where oak should have been. Smooth. Seamless. As if the door had never existed.

My palms pressed flat against it, searching. My breath caught. The wall was cold—colder than the fire should have allowed.

But the door was gone.

And—he was there.

I froze.

He did not move.

He stood between me and the only exit. Barefoot. Robed in black that wasn't fabric so much as shadow stitched together. He was tall. Too tall. Like he had been carved from cathedral pillars and set free.

His face was not beautiful.

It was brutal.

Scarred across one cheek. A split lip. Eyes that weren't eyes— just void. Two pits of black so deep I felt like I might fall into them and scream forever.

I recoiled.

Not from fear.

From recognition.

Because I knew, without being told, what he was.

Who he was.

He did not say a word.

He just stepped forward.

And the fire did not touch him.

Chapter Two

He did not move.

Not at first. Not even when I tore the silk from my thighs and let it burn in a heap at my feet. Not when I fell to my knees. Not when I gasped so loud it echoed and wept into my palms because the fire had not finished me. When I lifted my head, my vision blurring with the heat and tears he remained.

Standing there.

A towering vision of darkness.

The air changed when he entered it. Like silence made heavier. Like time folding in on itself. Like the walls no longer belonged to God, *only to him.* I kept my gaze down at first. I was afraid of what I'd see if I looked up. And more afraid of what he'd see if I didn't.

But my body betrayed me.

My eyes lifted before my breath caught. Before I could pray to something—anything—that he was just a shadow. A mistake. A hallucination formed from flame and fear.

He was none of those things.

He was real.

And he was watching me.

The fire cast gold along the stone floor but did not touch him. Not truly. It danced near him but never dared climb. His robes were black, darker than the smoke, frayed at the edges, and too still—like the air around him was afraid to move.

He was tall. Towering. Not like a man. Like a judgment. Shoulders broad enough to cast a shadow across the altar. Hands at his sides like weapons unused, not because they were dull but because he was patient.

His face was carved. Harsh. Silent. Not beautiful. Not broken.

Brutal.

One scar split his lip and dragged down his jaw like a forgotten vow. His cheek was marked, not slashed, but branded—some ruined echo of the sacred. And his eyes—

They weren't eyes.

They were void. Endless and black and depthless. No whites. No light. No pity.

I couldn't look away.

My first instinct was to crawl back. Not to escape him. But to make space between us. Because I wasn't sure what part of me he saw first—my shame or my survival.

But I didn't crawl.

I knelt.

Not because I was told.

Because something in the way he watched me made it impossible to do anything else.

The smoke coiled around us like incense at a false mass. The flames hissed near the rafters. Something wooden cracked above. Dust fell from the ceiling like old breath. Still, he didn't flinch.

He took one step forward.

And the fire bent away from him.

I gasped. Not because of him. Because of me. Because my thighs trembled when he moved. Because my mouth opened without command. Because some small, shivering girl still buried inside me whispered—

He's the one they meant.

They one who didn't speak.

He didn't have to.

His presence was language. His silence was scripture. His body, still and looming, said all the things the women never dared write down.

I was not meant to be saved.

I was meant to be seen.

He took another step.

I braced myself. For a blow. For a blessing. For a verdict.

He knelt.

And the world tilted.

He didn't kneel like a man. He didn't bow. He lowered himself with reverence, not to me, but to the act itself. Like kneeling was not submission. Like it was power. Like he controlled even gravity.

He sat still. Just opposite me. Legs folded. Hands resting on his thighs. Robes spilling like shadow.

He watched me.

He watched me like I was a ruin worth worshipping.

And I hated that I wanted it.

I wanted him to touch me.

Not because I was aroused.

Because I needed to know if I was real.

I wanted him to press his fingers into my jaw and tilt my face up like the women had. I wanted him to smear ash across my skin and call it holy. I wanted him to unmake the silence they had stitched into my spine and replace it with something that bled.

But he did nothing.

He only watched.

My breath caught on a sob I didn't let loose. My hands clenched the floor. My knees screamed. But I didn't move.

I met his gaze.

And something shifted.

Not in him.

In me.

I realized I wasn't waiting to be struck. I was waiting to be claimed.

And that was worse.

Because it meant I had already chosen him.

And he knew it.

He tilted his head, and his voice came like rusted iron—low, cracked, edged in smoke.

"You should have burned."

The words scraped across the inside of my chest.

I opened my mouth, but no answer came.

He took one breath. Measured. Deliberate.

"But you didn't."

My lips trembled. Not from cold. From truth.

He extended his hand.

Not to touch me.

To offer.

But I didn't move.

Because I knew—

If I reached back, I would not be offering consent.

I would be making a vow.

And I didn't know what it would cost.

He didn't lower his arm.

He didn't urge.

He just waited.

And I realized then that the fire had never been the test.

He was.

And I had already begun to fail.

Chapter Three

He didn't touch me.

He didn't have to.

His presence reached further than hands ever could. It slid beneath my skin, past the burns and the bruises and the places they tried to cauterize my want. He stayed knelt in the firelight, eyes on mine, hand outstretched.

Not demanding.

Not coaxing.

Just there.

And I stared at it like it held the knife that would either cut me open or free me. Like the weight of everything I used to be trembled at the edge of his palm.

I should have backed away.

I should have wept.

But all I could feel was the space between us.

The aching holiness of it.

My throat burned. My knees pulsed with blood. My lungs wouldn't obey. But none of it mattered. Because I hadn't moved. I hadn't run. And he was still waiting.

A second passed.

Then another.

Then—

I gave in.

Not out of surrender.

Out of inevitability.

My hand lifted before I knew I had made the choice. My fingers trembled in the space between us, caught on the last breath of who I was before him. I paused there—barely touching, barely real—and waited to be struck.

He didn't strike.

He didn't even flinch.

He simply closed his fingers around mine.

And the world dropped.

Not into pain.

Into silence.

Not the silence of the convent. Not the obedient hush they wrapped around our throats like veils. This was different.

This silence saw me.

This silence *pulled.*

He rose, taking me with him. Not forcefully. Just inevitably. Like he was gravity and I was a body too tired to pretend I belonged to anything else. I stood because he did. I breathed because his body made the air around me feel like something I could take in.

And when he turned, I followed.

He led me deeper into the chapel.

Past the altar. Past the crumbling pews. Past the places where girls before me had knelt and wept and been named or forgotten. I didn't know where we were going. I didn't care. I only knew the warmth of his hand, and the way it didn't pull or push.

It held.

He stopped before a stone slab at the far end of the room. It wasn't dressed like an altar. No cloth. No candles. Just cold stone, cracked and scorched at the edges. He turned to me. And for a moment, I thought he might speak.

He didn't.

He let go.

And still, I didn't run.

He gestured.

I understood.

I climbed onto the slab.

It was cold. My skin protested. My thighs shivered. I lay on my side at first, curled into the ache in my stomach, unsure if I was meant to kneel again or wait. But then—

"Lie on your back."

The words were quiet. Rough. Spoken like a man remembering how to speak for the first time in years.

I obeyed.

The stone stole my breath. My spine arched. My hair spread across the surface like ash, what little the fire left me. My arms trembled as I laid them by my sides.

He reached for something behind him. I didn't see what it was. But I heard it. Cloth. A thick, heavy piece. He draped it over me. Not to hide. To anoint. A wool blanket, scratchy against my skin, smelling of old fire and something darker.

The roughness was a different kind of touch. Each coarse fiber scraped against my burns like a tongue, like a thousand small prayers being written on my skin. It hurt. But the hurt felt sacred. Like penance turned inside out.

Like being touched everywhere without being touched at all.

It covered me from collarbone to thigh.

I expected him to leave me there.

He didn't.

He placed a hand on my ankle.

And I shattered.

Not because it hurt.

Because it didn't.

His palm was warm. Steady. Grounding. He didn't move it. Didn't slide it higher. Just let it rest, anchoring me to the stone, to the moment, to him.

"You lived," he said.

A statement. Not a praise. Not an accusation.

"They sent you to die, and you didn't."

I blinked up at the ceiling.

"Do you know what that makes you?"

My voice cracked.

"No."

His hand left my ankle. Traveled slowly, deliberately, to my hip. Still over the blanket. Still distant. But present.

"Mine."

The word hit harder than the fire.

It burned in a different way.

He leaned over me, his face passing through the flickering light. His breath stirred the hair near my ear. His eyes—those void-dark pits—held no lust.

Only ownership.

He brushed the blanket down, exposing my chest, my ribs, my stomach. My skin goose-pimpled in the cold, but I didn't shiver.

I ached.

Because he looked at me like I was scripture.

Like my body told a story only he had the right to read.

He placed one hand on my sternum.

Flat.

Heavy.

Claiming.

And I let him.

I didn't ask what came next.

I already knew.

It would be silence.

It would be obedience.

It would be him.

And I was ready.

I could feel the stone beneath me, grooved and burned with the memory of bodies that had come before mine. The cold sank in slow—up my spine, between my thighs, into the hollow curve just below my ribs. The wool blanket offered no comfort. It was a shroud. It smelled like him. Smoke and something older. Like breath held too long.

I didn't close my eyes.

I wanted to. I wanted to disappear into the dark behind my lids and pretend none of it was real. But he was still there. And I couldn't afford to miss him.

He stood beside the slab.

Still.

Not with hesitation. With intention. Like every second he made me wait was part of something sacred. Like my body needed to learn that silence wasn't absence—it was preparation.

I swallowed hard.

The movement made me aware of every part of myself.

My throat, raw.

My lips, cracked.

My skin, blistered faintly along the places where the fire kissed but did not consume.

He moved.

Not toward me.

Past me.

Into the darkness at the back of the chapel. A space I hadn't noticed. A low alcove, tucked behind a partial wall where the ceiling sagged and the fire hadn't dared touch.

I lifted my head, but only slightly. My wrists tensed. The instinct to follow nearly overtook me.

But I didn't move.

Because he hadn't told me to.

And somehow, that mattered more than the ache blooming in my chest.

A sound. Cloth. Water. The scrape of metal.

He returned carrying a basin.

It was simple. Iron, wide-brimmed, dented at the lip. It looked older than the chapel itself. Like it belonged in the ground, buried with bones and vow fragments.

He set it down beside me. I heard the water shift. No steam. No scent. Just the weight of it. Cold. I knew before he touched it to my skin. Cold like stone. Like truth. Like the space between what I was and what he would make me.

But when the cloth met my collarbone, the cold burned different. Not like fire—like baptism. Like being born backward. Each drop pulled heat from my skin until I couldn't tell where the burning ended and the cleansing began.

He knelt.

I wanted to look at him. I didn't.

Because if I saw his eyes, I might beg. And I wasn't sure what I'd be begging for.

He dipped a cloth into the water. Wringed it out slowly, precisely. Not like he was preparing to cleanse me.

Like he was about to anoint something holy.

He started at my collarbone.

The touch wasn't gentle. It wasn't rough.

It was sacred.

He didn't speak. Didn't explain. Just moved the cloth in slow circles, removing the ash, the oil, the scent of everything that wasn't him.

I breathed shallowly.

The cloth slid lower. Across my sternum. Between my breasts. Down my ribs. He didn't rush. He didn't linger.

But he saw me.

I could feel it in every pass of the cloth. In the way he adjusted the pressure. In the places he avoided—not out of shame, but precision.

Like he knew where the pain lived.

And wanted to leave it untouched until I was ready.

I felt tears burn behind my eyes.

But I didn't let them fall.

Because I didn't know what they were for.

Grief?

Relief?

The terror of being witnessed and not erased?

He reached my hips.

Paused.

I held my breath.

He lifted the cloth. Set it aside.

Then placed his hand over the blanket. Right above my belly. Heavy. Grounding.

"You are not unclean," he said.

His voice was a blade wrapped in velvet.

"You were *never* unclean."

I broke.

Not loudly.

But completely.

My hands curled into fists. My throat closed around a sob that felt like it had been living there since before I had a name. My body arched—not to resist, but to meet the weight of his truth.

He didn't comfort me.

He stayed.

His hand. His silence. His presence.

That was the comfort.

He stood.

I wanted to follow.

But I didn't.

Because stillness had become my offering.

He stepped behind me. I heard the basin shift. Water splash. Cloth wrung out once more.

He washed my thighs.

Not as a man.

As a priest.

Not to cleanse.

To remember.

He lifted one leg gently, bent it at the knee, and placed my foot flat against the slab.

He didn't part me.

He didn't touch the hunger.

He only pressed the cloth to the tender places.

And whispered,

"This is mine."

Not as a threat.

As a truth.

He covered me again.

And I wept.

Because I hadn't been touched.

Not truly.

But I had never felt more claimed.

I don't know how long I lay there. Time had become something else. Sacred. Suspended. Each breath stretched like a prayer I didn't know the words to.

The basin had gone still. The water quieted like it had never been moved. The fire had faded from the edges of the chapel, retreated to its shadows, licking only the walls it meant to leave blackened, not broken. And he—

He had gone quiet too. But not away. His silence pressed against my skin like a second washing. Like he was letting what he'd done to me settle. Letting his claim sink past flesh, past bone, into whatever part of me would remember this forever.

I could feel him.

Somewhere close. The weight of him without the weight. His presence throbbed in the air around me like a held breath, like a warning that didn't need a voice.

My skin was clean, but I didn't feel new. I felt exposed. As if the ash and silk had been my last defense, and now I lay beneath the weight of my own name, stripped of context.

Except I didn't know my name anymore.

Only the sound of his voice when he said *mine.*

My hands lay on my chest, folded like prayer. My thighs ached. My throat pulsed. My body was still.

Not from fear.

From understanding.

He returned with something in his hands.

I didn't look at first. I only heard the soft scratch of it against the stone. A brush of linen. A soft crackle.

Then the sound of a book opening.

Not a modern book.

One that breathed with every turned page.

A ledger.

Bound in cracked leather, dark as dried blood. The spine worn smooth from centuries of hands that had no right to touch it. When he opened it, the pages exhaled—a breath of ash and iron, of vows written in fluids thicker than ink.

Heavy enough to carry what it did. Heavy enough to carry me.

I turned my head.

He sat beside the slab, not touching me. Cross-legged, robes pooled around him like ash made solid. The book rested on his knees. His fingers brushed the pages like he was afraid of waking something.

"This is the record," he said. Low. Gravel rubbed through scripture.

"Not of sin. Not of blood. Of vows."

He turned another page.

The script was sharp. Black ink, carved in strokes too precise to be careless. No titles. No headings.

Just names.

Some were crossed out.

Some circled.

All final.

"They call it a ledger," he murmured. "But that implies debt."

He didn't look at me.

And somehow that made it worse.

"This isn't a balance."

His hand paused on a blank page.

I watched his throat move as he swallowed.

"It's a witness."

He set the quill to the edge of the parchment.

I couldn't breathe.

"What are you doing?" I whispered.

He didn't answer.

He wrote the first letter.

I felt it like a touch to my ribs.

The second.

A breath caught between my legs.

The third.

A cry in the back of my throat.

He finished the name.

My name.

Not the one the convent used.

Not the one my mother hissed like a curse.

The one I had never spoken aloud.

He said it.

Soft.

So quiet it almost didn't exist.

And yet it thundered inside me.

"Aven."

I sobbed.

It wasn't pain.

It wasn't joy.

It was recognition.

He closed the book. Bound it in black cloth.

And offered it to me.

Not like a gift.

Like a seal.

"If they ever ask who you are," he said, "show them this."

I reached for it with shaking hands.

Held it against my chest.

It was heavier than I expected.

But it didn't crush me.

It anchored.

"Why?" I asked.

His voice didn't change.

"Because I wrote you before the fire."

I stared at him.

I didn't ask how he knew.

I didn't need to.

Some truths don't need proof.

They just need to be spoken.

He reached out.

Pressed one finger to the center of my chest.

Right over the name he had just given back to me.

"You were never ash," he said.

"You were always the flame."

And I believed him.

I held that sentence inside me like it was a secret I hadn't earned. Not yet. Not fully.

Because I had never been the flame.

I had been the girl wrapped in oil. The girl waiting for the fire to choose her. The girl who thought burning would be the end.

But it hadn't ended me.

It had made space.

For this.

For him.

For the sound of my name spoken not like a curse, but a vow.

And for the first time, I didn't just believe it.

I began to carry it.

Not like ash.

Like heat.

Chapter Four

I DIDN'T SLEEP.

I couldn't. Not with the weight of my name pressed against my chest. Not with the shape of his voice still echoing behind my ribs. I held the book to my body like it might disappear if I loosened my grip.

He hadn't left.

But he hadn't touched me again either.

He knelt near the hearth where the fire had been coaxed into stillness. His hands rested on his thighs, palms up. He looked like a statue of something once feared and now forgotten—sacred and sharp, burned into history without explanation.

I watched him from the slab.

Naked beneath the wool.

Named.

Still not knowing what I belonged to.

He turned his head. Slowly. As if he'd felt me looking.

His eyes didn't search. They saw.

My breath caught.

He rose.

One motion. Soundless.

I sat up.

The book slid down my lap.

He didn't speak as he approached. He didn't need to.

Everything in me had already begun to answer him.

He stopped just before me.

Still towering.

Still robed.

But something in his expression had changed. Or maybe I had finally earned the right to see it. The restraint wasn't gone. It had just shifted. From control to offering.

He looked down at me. Then, with both hands, he undid the clasp at his throat.

The robe fell.

Not to the floor.

To his waist.

And I saw.

Not his body.

His history.

His chest was carved.

Lines. Curves. Marks I didn't understand. Some fresh. Some faded. Some raised in thick welts like they'd been reopened over and over until the skin no longer remembered smoothness.

Symbols.

Sigils.

Ritual script.

It didn't look like ink.

It looked like blood that refused to wash away.

I stared.

He let me.

Between his collarbones was the deepest one. A circle, broken at one end. Split open like a mouth. Or a wound. Lines radiated from it like a sun. Or a curse.

Beneath that, across his ribs, were smaller glyphs. I didn't know the language. But I felt it.

Felt what it cost him to carry them.

Felt what it meant to show them to me.

I slid off the slab.

The blanket fell.

I didn't care.

He didn't flinch.

He just waited.

I stood before him, bare.

Burned.

Named.

My hand rose. Slow. Unsteady.

I hovered just above the circle on his chest.

He breathed once. Shallow.

"What does it mean?" I whispered.

He looked down.

"This is where they vowed me to silence."

I swallowed.

"And this?" I asked, my fingertip grazing one mark below his ribs.

He didn't speak.

Just met my gaze.

Then said, "This is where I answered."

The air between us cracked.

Not with sound.

With knowing.

I leaned forward.

Pressed my lips to the first mark.

Not a kiss.

A benediction.

His breath caught.

My mouth moved to the next.

And the next.

I didn't know what I was doing.

Only that it felt right.

Like I was claiming him in the same way he had just claimed me.

When I reached the broken circle at his throat, I paused.

He tilted his chin up.

Offered it.

My lips brushed the center.

And I whispered,

"Let me vow it too."

His eyes snapped open.

Dark.

Shining.

Not with heat.

With reverence.

"You know what it means?"

I nodded.

"Say it," he said. "Or not at all."

I didn't look away.

I didn't hesitate.

"I vow silence."

His hand came to my throat.

Not to close it.

To feel the words live there.

"I vow obedience," I breathed.

His thumb pressed to the hollow of my neck.

"I vow to be claimed."

And then—

He kissed me.

Not my lips.

My throat.

Over the place where my vow had just taken root.

His mouth was fire and gravity and benediction all at once.

And I knew.

It wasn't about the words.

It was about who I became when I spoke them.

I closed my eyes.

And I let them become me.

Chapter Five

I had never been touched like this.

Not the way his hands came to me, not the way his eyes found my skin before his fingers did. He touched like he was speaking into me. Like his palms were pages and I was the last scripture he would ever be allowed to read.

He didn't hurry.

That would've been easier. If it had been urgent. If he'd been wild or frantic or overcome. But there was nothing frantic about the way he peeled the robe from his shoulders and laid it down on the stone for my back. Nothing careless in how he brushed my hair away from my eyes before lifting me—lifting me—onto the cloth, onto him.

My thighs ached from kneeling. My throat was raw from silence. My chest still wore the shape of the basin's cold. But none of that mattered. Not now. Not with the way he looked at me.

Like I had already been broken.

And he intended to build his vow from the pieces.

I lay back. Not in surrender. In offering.

He hovered over me. Bare-chested, his sigils catching what little light the chapel held, his skin marked with words I hadn't been taught to read. I didn't ask what they meant. I didn't need to. I felt them.

And I knew.

He was not here to take.

He was here to *claim*.

He braced his weight on one arm. His other hand found my wrist and lifted it. He didn't bind it. He didn't force it. He just guided it above my head. Then the other.

And I let him.

Because there was power in obedience when the choice was mine.

He pressed a kiss into the center of my palm.

Then lower.

To my breastbone. He licked my nipple until the skin puckered and want filled me.

To the soft dip of my stomach.

To the crease of my hip.

Each one a sentence.

Each one a vow.

When he moved over me, I felt the shape of him—hard, heavy, sacred.

My body arched.

I didn't mean for it to.

But I needed the weight.

I needed to be reminded I was still made of flesh.

"Look at me," he said.

I did.

He pushed forward.

Not all at once.

Just enough for my breath to catch and my mouth to fall open.

The stretch burned. It felt like something coming undone. Not pain. Not exactly. More like pressure. A deep pull in my core that said you were not meant to be empty forever.

He didn't move again until my body adjusted.

Until my hips tilted to take him deeper.

Until I said,

"*Yes.*"

It was the first word I gave him freely.

And it broke something in him.

He groaned. Low. Controlled. But not distant. Not detached. He sounded like a man praying through his teeth. Like he knew he wasn't just inside me—he was inside something holy.

He began to move.

Slow at first. A rhythm more reverent than erotic. His eyes stayed on mine. His body hovered. But his hips claimed.

Every thrust felt like worship.

Like he was driving his vow deeper into my marrow.

I didn't cry.

I moaned. Quietly. Like each sound was permission.

His hands gripped my wrists. Not hard. Just enough to anchor me.

I felt the chapel around us fall away.

The stone didn't bite anymore.

The fire didn't burn.

All that existed was this. Him. *The vow.*

He leaned down.

Pressed his lips to my throat.

"Mine," he said.

I arched beneath him.

"Say it," he demanded.

"Yours," I whispered.

"Louder."

"*Yours.*"

He slammed into me. Once. Hard. Deep.

And I gasped.

It wasn't pain.

It was recognition.

"Again," he said.

"Yours," I moaned.

"Even if I never let you go?"

"Yes."

"Even if I ruin you?"

"*Please.*"

He groaned into my throat.

And he began to fuck me in earnest.

No violence.

No rush.

Just deep, punishing reverence.

My legs wrapped around his waist.

My back arched off the cloth.

My mouth found his shoulder and bit.

And he didn't stop.

He kept moving.

Until I shattered beneath him.

Until the ache in my belly turned molten.

Until my body shook and I sobbed his name.

He came with a growl.

Low. Broken. Sacred.

And collapsed into me.

He didn't pull out.

He didn't speak.

He stayed.

His mouth at my ear.

His hands still at my wrists.

His breath matching mine.

"You're not my offering," he said.

I turned my face to his.

"Then what am I?"

He kissed me.

Not softly.

Not sweetly.

Just once.

And said,

"You are my vow made flesh."

Chapter Six

I DIDN'T EXPECT HIM TO STAY.

After everything—after his member split me open with reverence, after his vow spilled inside me like it had waited lifetimes—I thought he would pull away. Rise. Cloak himself again in those black robes that didn't just cover him, but contained him.

He didn't.

He stayed inside me.

Deep. Full. Still.

And the stillness was worse than the thrust.

Not because I wanted more.

Because I didn't know how to hold it.

My thighs trembled around his hips. My wrists had gone numb where he'd pinned them above my head. His breath was hot against my mouth, but he didn't kiss me. Just exhaled, slow, deliberate, like he was still saying something.

Or like he had said too much.

His heart beat against mine, steady and slow, and it didn't match my own.

Mine raced.

Because I had been ruined.

And I wanted him to ruin me again.

Not gently.

Not reverently.

I wanted his hunger.

I wanted the version of him that snarled scripture into my skin, not the one that stilled like prayer.

But I said nothing.

Because silence still lived in me.

He pulled back—only enough to look at me.

I met his eyes.

Black. Bottomless.

Still not hungry.

Still holy.

He reached up. Brushed a strand of hair from my cheek. Touched my lip where I'd bitten it.

"Sleep now," he said.

Sleep.

Like I could rest while my body still pulsed with the echo of him.

Like I could close my eyes while his cum still dripped from me like ritual.

But I obeyed.

Because obedience wasn't surrender anymore.

It was trust.

He cleaned me.

Again.

Without fanfare. Without heat.

A wet cloth. A reverent touch.

He didn't tease. Didn't trail fingers between my thighs to see if I ached. He already knew I did.

And that knowing was worse than the touch.

He laid me on the robe. Draped the blanket over my body.

Then he lay beside me.

Fully clothed.

His hands folded over his chest.

Close. Closer than I expected.

But not touching.

His thigh brushed mine once when I shifted.

I didn't flinch.

I turned toward him.

"Can I ask?" I whispered.

He opened his eyes.

"Yes."

"Why did you stay?"

He looked at the ceiling.

"Because you didn't run."

I swallowed.

"You thought I would?"

"They all do. *Eventually*."

I didn't ask who they were.

I didn't want to know.

He closed his eyes again.

"Do you want me to go?" he asked.

"No."

"Then sleep."

I did.

Eventually.

Not because I was safe.

Because I had never been so watched.

And the watching made me feel real.

I woke in silence, but it didn't feel empty.

It pressed into me.

Like a second skin, invisible and dense, steeped in breath I hadn't taken yet. I didn't open my eyes right away. I didn't need to. The weight of his presence was thicker than heat, thicker than stone, thicker than need. I could feel it at my back—constant, unmoving, held like a vow.

He hadn't left.

I could feel the tension in the air around us. Not because he touched me—he didn't—but because his restraint was a living thing. I could taste it.

Ash. Salt. Sweat. *Him.*

My body still ached from the night before, but it was a sacred ache. My body throbbed not with pain, but memory. Every breath dragged across the raw, holy place he'd carved into me. Not with violence. With reverence. With possession.

And I missed him inside me.

That thought hit me so suddenly I gasped. Quiet. Shame-laced. But true.

I missed the way his hips pressed into mine, the way his breath broke across my shoulder. I missed the press of his teeth, the scrape of his voice against my ear. I missed being filled.

I missed being kept.

My thighs pressed together and I let them. Let the friction spark against my slick, let the want rise in me again like a tide that refused to recede. I wanted him. Even now. Even still.

And that scared me.

Because I wasn't afraid of the ache.

I was afraid of what I'd become without it.

I opened my eyes slowly.

The chapel was still dim. Still half-shrouded in shadow and memory. The fire had burned low. The wax from the candle had run down onto the stone in thick, hardened trails. My limbs were heavy beneath the blanket, but I turned anyway.

He lay beside me.

Fully clothed.

Still.

Eyes closed.

Not asleep. He didn't sleep. I didn't believe he ever had.

But he was breathing. Barely.

As if to remind me that he was real.

And I wanted that reminder closer.

I shifted beneath the blanket.

The cloth pulled at the raw places between my legs. It made me hiss, but I didn't stop. I rolled onto my side, closer to him. Close enough to feel the heat that radiated from his body.

He still didn't move.

I reached for his wrist. Not to wake him.

To anchor myself.

My fingers barely brushed his skin.

He opened his eyes.

Void. Watchful. Awake.

He didn't flinch. He didn't ask.

He just looked at me.

And I said the only thing I could:

"Please."

His jaw tightened.

Not with rejection. With restraint.

I curled my fingers around his wrist.

"Please don't leave me alone with this," I said.

He turned fully then. His hand covered mine. Pressed it flat to his chest.

And for the first time, I felt his heart beat like it meant something.

It was steady.

Sacred.

Like scripture written in pulse.

"You're not alone," he said.

I shook my head.

"It's not just the silence. It's what you put in me."

He exhaled through his nose.

"I never meant to fill you," he said. "I meant to hollow you."

"Then why does it ache like I'm full of you?"

He didn't answer.

He didn't have to.

He pulled the blanket back from my shoulder.

And he looked at me.

Looked like he was deciding whether I was still sacred.

Whether I could take more.

Whether he should give it.

And whatever answer he found—

It broke him.

Because he leaned forward.

Pressed his mouth to my throat.

And whispered:

"Because I am still inside you."

I closed my eyes.

And let that be enough.

I didn't know if I was allowed to ask for it again.

The ache was there—alive beneath my skin, in the softest parts of me where his vow had taken root. But something about the silence between us felt different now. Not because it was colder. Because it was full. Like the chapel itself had learned to hold breath the way I held want.

He hadn't moved since he whispered into my throat. Since he reminded me that he hadn't left me—because he hadn't ever exited the place he carved inside me. He stayed close. Still not touching. But his presence was weight.

Not heavy.

Anchor.

I lay on my back, thighs drawn up slightly beneath the wool, breath slowing as I listened to him not speak. My pulse lived in strange places now. Between my ribs. Behind my knees. Deep inside me, where his cock had once pressed and filled and vowed.

It was terrifying, how much I missed it.

Not the pleasure.

The claim.

The way he didn't take me like he wanted to conquer something—but like I was already his and he was just proving it with every stroke.

I turned toward him. Slowly.

He was on his side, watching. Eyes open. Unblinking.

"You haven't slept," I said.

He shook his head.

"Do you ever?"

His voice was low.

"Not since they left me here."

I swallowed.

"And me?"

"You're not them."

There was a tension in his throat when he said it. A catch. Like the truth cost him.

"Then what am I?"

He reached out.

Just his fingertips.

They touched my mouth.

"Mine," he said.

I didn't blink.

"Then take me again."

His hand fell.

"You're still sore."

"I want it to hurt."

He exhaled through his nose.

"You don't know what you're asking."

"I do."

He didn't move.

So I did.

I rolled onto my stomach. Shifted my thighs apart. My ass lifted, still covered by the blanket. I didn't expose myself.

I offered.

I waited.

And he moved like a man unraveling.

The blanket was gone in a second. Tossed aside like it offended him. His hands landed on the curve of my ass with weight. He didn't caress. He gripped.

"You want it to hurt?" he said.

"Yes."

"Then don't run."

I didn't breathe.

I didn't speak.

I held still.

And he pulled my hips higher.

My knees pressed into stone. My forearms bent, forehead to the robe beneath me. The air against my opening made me shiver.

He spread me with both hands. Wide. Reverent.

"You're soaked," he murmured.

I whimpered.

He didn't tease.

He knelt behind me and pressed his cock to my entrance.

Not to slip in.

To wait.

"Say it," he said.

"*Yours.*"

He pushed.

Slow.

So slow.

The stretch burned. My mouth fell open. I gasped into the robe.

"All of it," he growled.

And he gave it to me.

Every inch.

His cock filled me like punishment. Like prayer. Like a blade I didn't know how to live without.

I cried out. Not because I couldn't take it.

Because I wanted more.

He fucked me then.

Not fast. Not gentle.

Savage.

Like he had waited to break.

His hands slid up my back. One found the back of my neck and pressed. The other gripped my hip so hard I knew it would bruise.

And I wanted it.

His teeth sank into my shoulder. Deep. I screamed his name. He growled into my skin, words I didn't understand.

Scripture.

Not spoken.

Carved.

He fucked me until I forgot what stillness was.

Until the world was only thrust and breath and the way his body made mine forget every hand that had touched it before.

He was snarling by the time I came. A ragged sound. Like possession.

Like worship.

I shattered.

And he followed.

He stayed inside me. Chest pressed to my back. Breath at my ear.

"You're not just mine," he whispered.

"You're the reason I remember I'm alive."

And I believed him.

He didn't pull out.

Not for a long time.

He stayed, cock still buried inside me, hand splayed across the back of my neck like he couldn't bear to let me forget where I belonged. His breath came in soft bursts against my spine, slower now, calmer—but not gentle. There was no gentleness in him. Only purpose. Only pressure.

And something else.

Ache.

I didn't expect it. I'd felt his hunger before, his control, his brutal reverence—but this was different. This wasn't about ownership. This was about need.

Not mine.

His.

I could feel it in the way his fingers twitched against my skin, in the way his hips stayed pressed against mine long after the last tremor of his climax had passed. It wasn't about the pleasure.

It was about not losing it.

Me.

Us.

Whatever vow we'd just sealed in sweat and bruises.

He shifted slowly, reluctantly, pulling out with a groan so low it vibrated through me. I collapsed forward, chest to stone, arms limp. His cum leaked from me in a slow, sacred spill, and I didn't try to stop it.

I wanted to be marked.

I wanted to be ruined.

He moved beside me, not speaking. Just breathing. His body still tense, still coiled like he didn't know if he could stop himself from taking me again.

I turned my head.

Watched him.

His jaw was clenched. His throat worked around something unsaid. His hand was fisted against the stone.

I reached for him.

He didn't flinch.

But his eyes met mine, and they were no longer void.

They were burning.

"Tell me," I whispered.

He shook his head.

"You have to."

"No," he said. Voice rough. "Because if I speak it, it becomes real."

"I want it real."

"You don't understand what that means."

I crawled closer. My body screamed at me, raw and aching, but I moved anyway. I climbed into his lap, straddled him, wrapped my arms around his neck.

He didn't touch me.

He let me come to him.

I pressed my forehead to his.

"I know what you are," I said.

He didn't answer.

"I know what you were made to do. I know what they took from you. I know you think this was about hollowing me."

He closed his eyes.

"But it wasn't," I whispered. "It was about making space. For you."

His hands came to my waist.

Tight. Shaking.

"If I love you," he said, the words like gravel, like ash, "I can't keep you."

"Then don't love me," I said. "Keep me anyway."

He exhaled hard, like the words punched something out of him.

I kissed him.

Not softly.

Not sweetly.

But true.

And he broke.

His arms wrapped around me. He crushed me to him. His mouth devoured mine. His teeth scraped my lip. His breath came ragged.

Not from arousal.

From surrender.

He laid me down again.

Not to take.

To hold.

And in that silence, I heard it for the first time.

He needed me, too.

Not because I was soft.

Not because I obeyed.

But because I let him fall without catching him.

And still came back to be broken again.

I thought I had already been taken completely.

That what he carved from me with his cock and his silence and his control was everything I had left. But as I lay there, trembling in the echo of what we'd done, I realized there was still something untouched.

Not my body.

My willingness.

And he saw it.

I don't know how, but he did.

He rose over me again like smoke given form. Not frantic. Not ravenous. Just certain. Like he had decided that if I stayed, if I really stayed, then I had to be taken again. Not just by his hands. Not just by his member. But by his hunger.

And God, I wanted it.

I rolled onto my side and reached for him. My hand found the edge of his robe, fingers curling into the rough fabric like I could anchor myself there. He looked down at me with that terrible stillness—his control so intact, so brutal, I could feel it pulsing in the air.

"Don't be gentle," I whispered.

His mouth didn't move. But I saw something fracture behind his eyes.

He dropped to his knees beside me.

His hands didn't tremble. But they were fast. Faster than reverence allowed. He pulled the robe from his shoulders like it burned him. And then he pulled the blanket from my body like I had no right to hide from him.

He flipped me onto my stomach.

My gasp echoed against the stone.

I didn't resist.

I arched.

Because I wanted it—wanted him—more than I wanted air.

He spread my legs with his knees. One hand at my hip. One pressed into the center of my back.

He didn't speak.

He bit.

Hard.

His teeth sank into my shoulder and I cried out—loud, raw, ruined.

His cock was thick and hard, pressing against my slit like it had been forged to live there. I was soaked. I could feel it slicking down my thighs. I knew he could smell it.

And he groaned like it hurt.

He pushed into me without warning.

Not slow.

Not soft.

Deep.

All of it.

My body jolted forward. My scream caught in my throat. He held me there, pinned, impaled. His cock stretched me open with a force that made my eyes blur.

He didn't let me adjust.

He fucked.

Brutal. Precise. Possessive.

His fingers tangled in my hair and yanked my head back. My spine arched. My mouth opened. I couldn't speak. Couldn't breathe.

"Say it," he growled into my ear.

"Yours," I gasped.

"Say what you are."

"Owned."

"Say who you belong to."

"You."

He fucked me harder.

His hips slammed into my ass, his balls slapped against my soaked pussy, and still it wasn't enough. I clawed at the stone, my nails scraping raw, my insides squeezing him so tight I could feel every inch, every ridge, every groan he bit back.

"This body is mine," he said. Voice low. Ragged.

"Yes," I sobbed.

"Say it."

"It's yours."

"Louder."

"It's yours."

He bit my neck. My shoulder. The curve of my back.

He marked me with teeth and scripture and ruin.

And when I came, it was like burning alive. My pussy pulsed around his cock, my scream echoed through the chapel, and I didn't care who heard.

He followed.

His roar wasn't human.

It was holy.

He spilled inside me like he was branding me with his cum. Filling me until I couldn't remember a time I hadn't belonged to him.

He collapsed over me.

Still inside.

Still hard.

Still his.

And I whispered, not because I needed to be heard, but because it was truth:

"I never wanted gentleness. I wanted you."

He kissed the back of my neck.

And stayed.

The ache didn't leave.

It lingered like a bruise under my skin, like the echo of his growl in the hollow of my throat. He had filled me so completely I couldn't tell where I ended and he began. But it wasn't enough. It would never be enough. Because every time he took me, he didn't just fuck me—he rewrote me.

I lay on my side, sweat cooling on my skin, his cum leaking from between my thighs in a slow, revenant drip. The bruises he left across my hips were already darkening, his bite marks pulsing like sacred sigils carved in flesh. I wore them like scripture.

He sat at the edge of the robe, half-dressed, head bowed. His back rose and fell with measured breath, but I knew he wasn't calm. I could feel the storm in him, held down by discipline he no longer needed to wear.

Because I wasn't running.

I never would.

"You didn't hold back," I whispered.

He didn't look at me.

"You didn't ask me to."

"You liked it."

"That doesn't mean it was safe."

I sat up. My thighs trembled. My pussy ached. My lungs stretched around his name even when I didn't speak it.

"I don't want safe."

He turned.

His face was drawn, mouth hard, eyes ruined.

"What do you want, then?"

I crawled to him.

Slow.

Deliberate.

I settled in his lap, naked, raw, shameless.

"I want what you left inside me," I said. "The part you think you can fuck out of me and still walk away clean."

He didn't move.

His hands hovered at my waist.

"You want my need."

"No," I said. "I want the part of you that broke when I didn't break."

His throat worked.

He gripped my hips and pressed his forehead to my sternum. Not reverent. Not weak.

Wrecked.

"I was supposed to hollow you," he whispered. "That was the vow. The only purpose I had left."

I cupped his jaw, forced his gaze up.

"You did."

His mouth trembled.

"Then why does it feel like salvation?"

"Because it is."

He pulled me against him like he meant to pray.

Like he meant to undo the prayer he'd already spoken too loud.

We didn't fuck again.

We stayed like that. Held. Sweating. Breathing.

And I felt it. The shift.

He didn't want to ruin me anymore.

He wanted to be ruined by me.

And he already was.

Chapter Seven

He didn't touch me the next day.

Not once.

Not when I woke beside him on the stone, bruised and slick with the memory of his mouth. Not when I stretched, wincing at the delicious pull between my legs, hoping his breath might hitch when I did.

Not when I stood.

Not even when I walked across the chapel, bare, to the basin. When I cupped water in my palms and let it fall over my skin like I remembered his fingers had done.

He just watched.

He always watched.

But this time, it wasn't with heat.

It was with reverence.

And it felt like absence.

I dressed in silence. Not because he asked me to, but because I couldn't bear the way his gaze held me when I was naked. Like I was scripture he'd already read too many times and couldn't bring himself to deface again.

When I tied the shift at my waist, I thought he'd move. Come to me. Drag it down my arms and remind me what it meant to be claimed.

He didn't.

He turned away.

And it broke something in me I didn't know was still unbroken.

I sat at the edge of the altar, feet bare, toes curling against the cold stone.

I waited.

For his voice.

For his hand.

For the press of his body behind mine.

But all I got was silence.

And I hated it.

Not because it was cold.

Because it made me feel like a relic. Like something once holy and now shelved.

I wanted him to fuck me again.

No, that wasn't it.

I wanted him to need it.

I wanted to see him lose the discipline he wore like skin. I wanted to watch him snap his vows against my ribs and mark me again. I wanted to feel his hand at my throat, not because he had to silence me, but because he couldn't bear to hear me say I belonged to anyone else.

But he stayed seated. Cross-legged on the floor, eyes half-lidded like prayer.

So I spoke.

"Did I do something wrong?"

His eyes opened.

They found me instantly.

And I regretted asking.

Not because it wasn't true.

Because of how long it took him to answer.

"No," he said. Simple. Final.

But his voice lacked the bite I'd come to crave.

It felt like a door closing.

I slid off the altar.

Walked to him. Stood over him. Let him see what he hadn't touched. The lines of my legs. The faint bruises across my collarbone.

"Then why are you looking at me like that?"

"Like what?"

"Like I already left."

He didn't blink.

He just breathed.

And I hated him for it.

Because I wanted to scream. I wanted to bleed. I wanted to crack open and show him the hollow he put there and ask why he wasn't crawling inside.

But I didn't.

Because I still knelt.

Even when I stood, I still knelt.

So I turned away.

And this time, he didn't stop me.

I thought if I left the altar, I might feel different.

Less sacred. Less watched.

Less unwanted.

But the chapel followed me, no matter where I walked. The stones had memory. The air had weight. I could still feel the shape of his cock inside me, the echo of his breath at my ear. I sat beneath the ruined window, knees drawn up, arms around them, trying not to unravel from the silence.

He hadn't moved.

He hadn't spoken.

But I could feel his presence behind me, burning a path down my spine.

I hated the ache it left.

I hated that I missed him already. That my thighs clenched for him. That my breath stuttered when I remembered the sound of his voice growling scripture against my skin.

But what I hated most—

Was that I wanted him to stay away.

Because I didn't know who I was when I wasn't being ruined.

I dug my nails into my knees. Pressed hard enough to hurt. Maybe if I bruised myself first, he wouldn't need to. Maybe if I shattered before he touched me again, I'd get to decide what pieces were left.

I didn't hear him move.

But I felt it.

The shift in the air. The weight. The way the silence cracked just enough to make room for him.

He came to stand in front of me. I didn't look up.

"You're kneeling," he said.

"No," I whispered. "I'm hiding."

He knelt slowly. His hand came to rest against the floor beside mine. Not touching. Just there.

"There is no hiding in this place."

I looked up.

His face was close. His mouth soft. His eyes still void, but not empty.

"Then what do I do with the ache?"

His throat worked.

"You speak it."

I closed my eyes.

And I said it.

"I don't know who I am if you're not taking me."

The words broke something between us.

Not the tension.

The control.

His breath caught. His hand rose. Not to touch me. To press to his own mouth.

Like he wanted to swallow the sound of me.

"I want more," I whispered. "But not because I'm afraid. Not because I need to be ruined. Because I want to belong to the man who watched me burn and still said I was worth saving."

He reached for me.

Slow. Careful. Like I was flame now. Not ash.

His fingers brushed my cheek.

"Then vow it," he said.

I nodded.

I unfolded. Rose to my knees.

I placed my hands over his chest.

And I said it.

"I vow not to run. Not even from the quiet."

His eyes closed.

"I vow to stay, even when I'm not being touched."

His breath broke.

"I vow to want you. In silence. In stillness. In the ache."

And when his eyes opened again, I saw it.

Not hunger.

Not possession.

Worship.

"Then we begin again," he said.

And I knelt.

Not to submit.

To be chosen.

Again.

He didn't touch me after I vowed.

Not because he didn't want to. I could feel it in the air between us—the way his body tensed when I breathed too deeply, the way his gaze lingered on my lips like they were the only place he wanted to put his hunger. He watched me like a man drowning watches the surface. But still, he didn't reach.

I stayed kneeling long after the words left my mouth.

I didn't want to move.

The silence was no longer unbearable.

It was heavy. Sacred. Full of him.

I could feel his restraint coiling through the stillness like a second vow. One he made without sound. One I wasn't sure he knew he was making.

He stood.

I stayed.

He walked away. Not far. Just to the altar.

He placed both palms against it like it had spoken to him. Like it asked something of him. His shoulders were tight beneath the frayed linen of his robe, his breath shallow. The marks on his back peeked out from the loose collar. Rigid scars. Raised scripture. Each one a sentence carved into skin.

I wanted to trace them.

I wanted to kneel behind him and press my mouth to every one.

Instead, I waited.

He turned after a long stretch of silence. His eyes found me immediately.

He didn't ask me to rise.

But his hand reached out. Just a little.

I stood. Walked to him. Slowly. Every step echoing like confession.

He didn't touch me.

He took my hand and placed it on his chest.

Bare skin. Warm. Beating.

Not fast.

But not calm.

His heart spoke in stutters. In sentences I didn't know how to translate.

"Do you feel it?" he asked.

I nodded.

"It's not fear," he said.

"I know."

"It's not control."

"Then what?"

His hand covered mine.

Pressed it harder against him. Into him.

"It's what I haven't given anyone."

I looked at him.

Really looked.

And I saw it.

He wanted to be ruined.

Not just as an offering. But as a man who never believed he deserved to be touched without command.

I stepped closer.

Our bodies almost touching.

His breath caught.

I leaned in. Pressed my lips to his sternum. Felt his heart hammer harder.

"Let me take it," I whispered.

He shook his head.

"You already did."

And then he stepped back.

Not away.

Just far enough to breathe.

I didn't chase him.

Because I didn't need to.

He had already followed me into silence.

And now it was his turn to ask for more.

It was the way he turned his back to me that undid me.

Not the silence. Not the restraint. Not the distance.

But that small, brutal act of denial.

He walked to the far edge of the chapel and sat on the lowest stair of the altar. His shoulders hunched, hands between his knees, head bowed like the weight of wanting had finally bent him. And still, he said nothing.

I stood in the same place. Barefoot on cold stone. Still damp between my legs from the last time he took me. Still marked by his teeth. Still wearing the bruise of his hand like it was jewelry.

And none of it called him back to me.

My stomach twisted.

Not from rejection.

From grief.

Because I saw him. Not just the enforcer. Not the ruin. Not the man who'd hollowed me.

I saw the man who hadn't spoken aloud what he wanted since the Order stripped it from him.

And I saw how close he was to losing what little voice he had left.

I crossed the floor without sound.

The stones were cold, the air colder. The sky had darkened behind the high windows, casting the chapel in bruised light. He didn't look up when I knelt beside him.

But he knew I was there.

I didn't reach for his hand.

I reached for the hem of his robe.

Not to pull it away.

To hold it.

To remind him I knew where to kneel.

He shifted. Not toward me. But like he couldn't decide if he should pull away completely.

"Why won't you speak it?" I asked.

His jaw worked.

I waited.

And then, after too long, he said:

"Because if I do, I won't stop."

"Then don't stop."

He looked at me.

And there it was.

The thing he never let me see.

Not heat.

Not pain.

Devotion.

Not the kind wrapped in scripture. Not the kind preached through ritual.

The kind that bled.

He stood so quickly the fabric tore where I held it.

I didn't flinch.

He walked to the wall. Pulled something from behind the altar.

A book.

Not the ledger.

His.

Worn leather. No markings.

He brought it to me and dropped it at my knees.

"Read it," he said.

I opened it.

The pages were filled with small, slanted script. Not neat. Not sacred.

Personal.

It was rage and longing and fragments of prayer so broken I couldn't tell where the sin ended and the want began.

He never used names.

Only one word repeated, over and over, across nearly every page:

Her.

And then I found it.

A passage so sharp it cut just to read:

If I were capable of love, it would have been her.

I didn't cry.

I closed the book.

Looked up at him.

"You are."

His chest rose.

Once. Shallow.

He knelt in front of me.

Took the book from my lap.

Set it aside.

His hands came to my waist.

And this time when he pulled me into his lap, it wasn't to fuck me.

It was to hold me like the only thing he still believed in.

His mouth pressed to my shoulder.

And he whispered:

"I was never meant to survive you."

And I answered:

"Then die in me."

And he did.

Not in flesh.

In vow.

In silence.

In surrender.

I didn't want sleep.

I wanted to be touched. Again. Differently.

I wanted to be kept.

But not with bruises this time. Not with bite marks or binding or vows carved into the soft places between my thighs. I wanted his breath in my mouth. I wanted the hush that came not after fucking—but during. That unbearable stillness when two bodies stopped moving but didn't stop needing.

I lay on the robe, curled on my side, watching him. The fire had long since burned low. Shadows flickered across the floor like hands reaching for something they would never hold.

He hadn't left me. He hadn't risen.

But he hadn't touched me again either.

He was breathing harder than he should have been. Like the restraint had cost him. Like every second he stayed seated and not inside me pulled skin from his bones.

I turned to him slowly.

"Are you punishing me?"

His head lifted.

"No."

"Then why does this feel like silence I haven't earned?"

He stood. Crossed the room.

He didn't answer.

Just knelt.

One knee between mine. One hand at my throat.

Not pressing.

Just reminding.

"Because I want to be gentle."

His voice scraped across the top of my chest.

"But I don't know how."

I blinked.

And whispered,

"Then let me teach you."

He stilled.

Something in him faltered.

And I saw it.

The fear.

Not of me.

Of softness.

Because it didn't have rules. Because it didn't come with vows. Because it wasn't something he could fuck or bleed or worship into obedience.

But he nodded.

And when he kissed me, it was different.

Not less.

Just slower.

He undressed me with hands that didn't tremble but hovered— like every part of me was still his altar.

He laid me down and spread my thighs without force. Without ritual.

Just want.

His mouth moved down my chest, over my stomach. He didn't speak.

He didn't need to.

When his tongue found my slit, I cried out.

Not because it was rough.

Because it was worship.

He licked me slow. Deep. Like he was memorizing me.

Like I was the last sacred thing he would ever be allowed to taste.

His tongue fucked me while his hands held my hips still, and I sobbed into the stone. My thighs shook. My back arched. And when I came, it wasn't shattering.

It was surrender.

He kissed the inside of my thigh and crawled up my body.

He didn't speak.

He slid his cock inside me in one long, slow thrust.

And I cried again.

Because it didn't hurt.

It healed.

He fucked me like he wanted to live there. Like my body was the only place he'd ever felt whole.

His hand found my jaw. Tilted it. His lips touched mine.

Not a kiss.

A binding.

And when he came, he didn't growl.

He breathed my name like a secret.

And I knew.

He didn't need to vow anymore.

Because now, I was the vow.

He stayed inside me long after the heat faded.

Not moving. Not speaking. Just breathing into the soft space where my neck met shoulder, like the rhythm of my pulse was the only sound he trusted not to betray him.

I didn't know how to hold it.

The quiet. The weight of his body against mine. The feel of his cock still buried deep, not in conquest now, not even in worship —but in something I hadn't been taught to name. Something slow. Terrible. Precious.

I turned my head into his hair. Let it tangle in my lips. He smelled like salt and sleep and fire that had burned too long. His weight crushed me in the best way—heavy, grounding, the kind of pressure that didn't restrain but reminded.

You are here.

You are still wanted.

You are kept.

I closed my eyes and listened.

To the chapel.

To his breath.

To the silence between us that felt less like absence now and more like promise.

He shifted only when I did, when my leg twitched around his hip, when my fingers curled at his spine.

He slid out of me with a low groan that made my skin tighten, my body ache all over again. His warmth spilled down my thigh in a slow, thick slide. I felt ruined. Filled. Unmade.

And loved.

Though he would never say it.

He sat beside me, back against the altar, chest bare, robes discarded somewhere in the dark.

I pulled the blanket over me, not out of shame.

Just to stay close to the warmth of him.

He spoke without looking at me.

"I was made to undo."

His voice was rough. Low. Thicker than usual.

"I was made to carve women into silence. To take the parts of them that remembered how to want and smother them in stone and scripture. I didn't fuck. I broke. And it worked."

He paused.

I said nothing.

"Until you."

He turned his head then.

Looked at me with eyes no longer void.

Eyes full.

"You didn't just kneel. You stayed."

"Because you didn't lie," I whispered.

"I didn't want to want you."

"Then why did you touch me like that?"

He didn't blink.

"Because I never knew how to love anything that didn't flinch."

The air left my lungs.

Not from shock.

From truth.

I crawled to him. Slow. Bare beneath the blanket. My knees dragging across the stone. I climbed into his lap and wrapped myself around him like silence itself. My head on his shoulder. My mouth at his throat.

"Then let me teach you how to keep what doesn't run."

He held me.

All of me.

Without asking for the vow.

And that was the vow.

That was everything.

<h1 style="text-align:center">Chapter Eight</h1>

I WOKE TO COLD STONE AND ABSENCE.

Not silence—absence. The kind that crept beneath the ribs and whispered something sacred had moved. The kind that made me feel like I'd been left in the mouth of something that no longer wanted to swallow.

He wasn't beside me.

The heat from his body had already faded.

I reached out to the place where his chest had pressed against my back, where his hand had cupped my waist in the half-sleep of after, and felt only stone.

The blanket had slipped down my spine. My thighs were bare. His cum had dried between them, sticky and soft like a second skin. I didn't wipe it away.

I rose slowly, each muscle stretching into ache, each bruise humming beneath the weight of what he'd made me. Not just what he'd done.

What he'd made me.

No candles burned. No fire cracked. The chapel breathed a different kind of quiet—thicker, older. The kind that waits.

I pulled his robe over my body. It hung from my frame like it recognized me. Like it had draped the shoulders of every woman who had come before me. I didn't like the way that thought settled in my stomach.

I walked barefoot across the nave.

No sound.

No movement.

I didn't call for him.

I let the chapel guide me. Past the altar. Around the basin. Toward the low arch at the back wall I had never crossed.

The shadows thickened here. Like memory lived in the dust. Like breath had been held too long.

I stepped down into it.

And I found the book.

It was resting on a stone ledge, spine cracked, corners curled. No cloth. No bindings. Just leather worn soft from hands that hadn't known gentleness.

I didn't hesitate.

I opened it.

The first pages were blank. Then stained. Then—

Names.

Hundreds of them.

Some full. Some just initials. A few scratched over so violently the page had torn. Others circled. Underlined. Dated.

There were no explanations. No titles. No context.

Just ink and violence.

And then I found mine.

Aven.

Written not in gold.

Not in red.

In black.

The stroke was hard. Deep. Like he hadn't wanted to write it but had known he must.

There was no circle around it.

No line through it either.

Just a blank space beside it.

Waiting.

For what?

I didn't want to guess.

I turned the page.

More names.

Different hand. Older. Shaking.

And then—

One I knew.

Amare.

Not just written.

Crossed out.

Twice.

I stared at it like it might reach up from the page and strike me. Like the weight of it might be enough to pull the air from my lungs.

She had been here.

Not metaphorically. Not whispered. Not guessed.

She had been here. She had knelt. She had been written.

And then erased.

My mother.

The one who wrapped silence around my throat like ribbon.

The one who never told me where I came from.

The one who pushed me through the chapel doors without trembling.

She had been here.

And she hadn't survived it.

I sat down slowly.

Right there in the dust. Robe tucked around my legs. The book open in my lap like it might bite if I closed it too fast.

The chapel felt different now.

Less sacred.

More true.

He hadn't told me.

He had known.

And he hadn't told me.

I ran my fingers over her name. The ink flaked beneath my touch. The line through it was final. Harsh. Unforgiving.

She hadn't been forgotten.

She had been removed.

And I—

I was what they sent next.

The girl who looked like her.

The girl who burned like her.

But didn't break.

I closed the book.

And I didn't cry.

Because it didn't hurt.

It clarified.

I wasn't the first.

But I would be the last.

I carried the book like it was breathing.

Its weight felt different now. Heavier. More intimate than flesh, more brutal than chain. I didn't need to open it again to feel her name beneath my fingers. Amare. My mother. Crossed out. Twice. A name not lost but exiled.

It wasn't grief I felt.

It was inheritance.

It was the echo of a vow she couldn't finish pulsing like blood behind my teeth.

I didn't look for him.

I didn't need to.

He was already watching me.

He stood in the doorway of the alcove, half-shadowed, arms loose at his sides like they didn't know whether to hold or hurt. His robe hung open. His throat was bare. The mark above his heart was visible—the broken circle, carved not with ceremony but survival.

He didn't speak. He just looked at me like he was waiting to see what I would do now that I knew. Now that I'd seen what he never said.

I rose slowly.

Carried the book with both hands.

Held it out to him.

He didn't take it.

He stared at it. At me. At what it meant to be seen holding it.

"She was here," I said.

His jaw tensed.

"Before me."

He didn't nod.

He didn't blink.

He just said, "Yes."

I stepped closer.

"You knew."

"I did."

"And you didn't tell me."

He exhaled slowly, like the breath had been waiting for years.

"Because it was never supposed to matter."

"She was my mother."

"She was an offering."

The words hit harder than any lash.

He didn't say them cruelly. That made it worse.

He said them like they were fact. Like she had never been anything else.

I stepped forward again. Pressed the book to his chest.

He didn't move.

"Do you remember her?" I asked.

His eyes darkened.

Not with anger.

With ache.

"No," he said. "Just her name."

I lowered the book.

"She survived."

"Not the way you did."

I studied him.

He didn't look away.

"What did she do?" I whispered.

"She begged."

"For what?"

"To forget. To disappear. To not be touched."

I swallowed.

"And me?"

He stepped forward.

Took the book from my hands.

Set it aside.

Then placed his hands on either side of my face.

"You didn't beg at all."

His thumbs traced my cheekbones.

Not gently.

Precisely.

"You asked to be hollowed."

I nodded.

"You stayed."

His mouth was close. So close I could feel the vow he wasn't speaking hanging between us like heat.

I looked at him.

Not the ruin. Not the keeper. Not the priest.

Just the man who remembered.

"My mother begged to forget," I said.

He didn't nod.

He didn't flinch.

He just let it sit between us like scripture too heavy to carry.

"And me?" I asked, voice low, deliberate.

His breath faltered.

"You begged to be remembered."

The air tightened.

My fingers curled around the spine of the book still cradled in my hands. I stepped forward. Pressed it to his chest. Not to accuse.

To be *answered*.

"Then say it," I whispered. "Say I was never hers."

His jaw locked. His gaze flicked to my mouth like the words were already there.

And then—

He leaned in.

Mouth to ear.

Voice like a blade drawn through old parchment:

"You were mine before the fire."

I didn't gasp this time.

I *burned*.

Not with pain.

With memory.

With truth I had already known but hadn't dared wear.

I pulled back, just enough to see his eyes.

"Then write me again," I said. "Not in the ledger."

I reached for his hand.

Pressed it to the place just below my ribs.

"Write me in you."

He didn't answer.

He didn't need to.

Because I already had.

Night crept into the chapel like breath slipping from between parted lips. It didn't announce itself. It just filled the space we hadn't touched. The stone turned colder. The air stilled. And the silence began to feel heavier than it had in days.

He sat across from me now.

Not close. Not far.

He'd lit no candles. Made no fire. And I hadn't asked.

Somehow, the darkness suited what hovered between us. Not shame. Not guilt. But recognition. Of what we'd taken. Of what had been taken before us. Of the ledger still breathing in the corner like a wound left open too long.

I didn't sleep. I knew he wouldn't either.

I pulled the robe tighter around my body, even though it smelled like him. Especially because it smelled like him. It clung to my skin like memory, like ruin. Like a thing I wasn't supposed to want anymore.

But I did.

God, I did.

Not just his cock. Not just his voice. Not even his hands.

I wanted the weight of him against my back.

I wanted to be split open again, not because I needed to be broken—but because I wanted to feel something louder than silence.

I wanted to be reminded.

That I hadn't been erased.

That I had been chosen.

His breath shifted across the room.

I heard him rise.

But I didn't move.

I didn't have to.

His steps were slow. Measured. Every one of them closer.

And when he stopped behind me, I didn't turn.

I whispered,

"She never stayed, did she?"

He didn't speak.

But I felt it. The way his silence sharpened.

"My mother."

He breathed in. Once. Held it.

Then exhaled the truth.

"She begged to forget."

I nodded.

"And me?"

His fingers brushed my jaw.

Lifted my face.

"You begged to be remembered."

I turned then.

Faced him.

And saw the wreckage beneath the stillness. The way his mouth twitched like it wanted to speak more than it should. The way his hands hovered like they wanted to worship but didn't know where to begin.

"I never meant to be kept," I said.

"You weren't."

"Then what am I?"

His voice cracked when he said it.

"You're the vow I never said aloud."

I stepped closer.

"Say it now."

He stared at me.

"I can't."

"Why?"

"Because if I do, you'll hear it everywhere."

"And?"

His breath faltered.

"And I want it to belong to you."

I touched his chest.

Pressed my fingers to the mark carved there. The one that split the broken circle. The one that hadn't bled in years.

"It already does," I whispered.

He kissed me then.

Not like the others.

Not to break.

Not to brand.

But to remember.

And I let him.

Because I knew now.

I had never been just an offering.

I was the echo he had waited to become.

And he had always been my answer.

He wrote my name again.

But not in the ledger.

Not in the book that breathed with forgotten girls, with lines through names and circled sentences of obedience. He wrote it on the floor. With chalk. With blood. I don't know which. I didn't ask.

Because the moment I saw it, I dropped to my knees.

Not because I was told.

Because I wanted to see what it looked like from the place I had first belonged to him.

He stood behind me, silent.

But the silence wasn't empty.

It was full of reverence. Of need. Of a ritual he hadn't spoken but had already begun.

The circle wrapped around the letters of my name, drawn unevenly, with lines that trembled like even the stone couldn't believe I had survived this long.

He crouched beside me.

Placed a hand at the center of my back.

Not to push.

To anchor.

"Say it," he murmured.

I closed my eyes.

Breathed in the dust.

And said it.

"My name is Aven."

His hand flexed.

"I was sent here to be erased."

His breath caught.

"But I stayed."

He lowered his head to mine.

"Because you weren't a sacrifice."

"What was I, then?"

"A vow I hadn't written yet."

I turned my head.

Found his mouth.

Kissed him.

It wasn't soft. It wasn't savage.

It was scripture.

His hands slid down my spine, beneath the robe, until they found the backs of my thighs. He lifted me without effort, without hesitation, and laid me down in the center of the circle.

My name beneath me.

His body above me.

The altar wasn't behind us.

I was the altar now.

He didn't fuck me with urgency.

He moved with reverence. Every thrust slow, deep, exact. Like he was carving something into me with the length of his cock, like he was sealing a spell that had waited too long.

My legs wrapped around him before I realized they had moved. My hands found his back, traced the scars I couldn't name, the ones that didn't belong to me but somehow had always meant to find me.

He whispered into my neck.

Not words.

Sounds.

Broken fragments of something that might have once been holy.

My hips tilted up, met him. Matched him. Became him.

And I said it again.

"My name is Aven."

His hand gripped my jaw.

"Say it louder."

I screamed it. *"MY NAME IS AVEN!"*

He came undone.

And when he finished inside me, shaking, swearing, whispering things I'll never repeat, he looked down at me and said:

"Now it's written."

I touched his face.

And answered:

"Then never erase me."

His eyes closed.

"I couldn't."

I lay there, wrapped in him, pressed into the shape of the name he had given back to me.

And knew:

He had never claimed me.

He had only remembered where I belonged.

Chapter Nine

I woke to warmth and absence.

Not the suffocating kind, not the kind that scraped against the walls of my chest like a scream. This was different. This was silence with breath still inside it. Like he had only just left.

The robe he had wrapped me in the night before was still damp with our sweat. I didn't push it off. I pulled it tighter. Drew it against my body like it could hold the shape of his chest a little longer. The place between my legs was tender, slick, aching in a way that felt less like aftermath and more like memory.

And beneath that ache was the certainty: he would touch me again.

Not because he had to.

Because he couldn't help it.

But he wasn't there now.

And I felt the shape of his absence more acutely than I expected.

The chapel was quiet. Still dark in places where the light hadn't yet returned. But it was not untouched.

Someone had placed a folded cloth beside me. Clean. Warm.

A small basin of water. A strip of linen. A piece of bread wrapped in waxed paper.

And there—beside it all—was my robe.

Folded.

Deliberately.

Like reverence.

Like he had touched it after I slept, and wanted me to know he had handled it not as clothing, but as skin.

I didn't cry.

But I almost did.

Because there was something more brutal about this than any of the times he'd pinned me down. Something more intimate than the teeth he'd buried in my shoulder. Something I didn't know what to do with.

Care.

Not romance.

Not tenderness.

But attention.

He had seen me at my most obscene. Spread. Dripping.

Screaming beneath him. And now he had left me wrapped in silence, fed, clothed, covered.

Not discarded.

Kept.

I sat with that truth—wrapped in his robe, the smell of him still clinging to my skin like benediction.

He had touched every part of me, carved silence into my body with his hands and his vows—and still, he had left me covered.

Not discarded.

Preserved.

And that was worse.

Because it meant he thought I might break now that I had finally been kept.

But I wouldn't.

I didn't want to be devoured.

I wanted to *remain*—even if it meant staying whole was harder.

So I stayed.

Not because he would return.

But because I would meet him in the stillness, again and again, until he learned that reverence could last longer than ruin.

I rose slowly, knees stiff, thighs raw. My pussy still pulsed from the last time he'd been inside me. I liked it. I wanted it to stay sore. To throb when I breathed too hard or shifted too quickly. I wanted to remember.

I cleaned myself. Quietly. The water was cold, but I didn't flinch.

I tore the bread with my fingers. Let it dissolve on my tongue. It was rough, dry, a little sweet. I imagined him making it. Not kneading, not baking. Just preparing it in silence, the way he prepared me. With purpose.

I dressed.

The robe smelled like him.

Ash. Iron. Skin.

I didn't tie it closed.

Let it fall open down the center. Let the air kiss my chest, my ribs, the curve of my belly. I wanted him to see that I hadn't hidden the marks. That I hadn't erased what he left behind.

I stepped out into the chapel slowly.

He wasn't there.

But I felt him.

The place still carried his weight. The walls breathed it. The floor ached with it. I walked past the altar, past the basin, into the light where the windows bled color.

And I knew he was watching.

Even if I couldn't see him.

He was watching the way I moved now.

Not because he needed to punish me.

Because I had become a thing worth witnessing.

And I knew then—

He didn't stay away to protect me.

He stayed away because he was still learning how to keep me without breaking me.

And I wanted him to learn it.

Slowly.

With me.

Only me.

I found him where I knew he'd be.

Kneeling before the altar like his body was an apology. Not to me. Not even to God. Just to the stone. As if the floor itself remembered how he'd once broken someone there. As if it might forgive him for how he hadn't broken me.

He was bare from the waist up.

His back to me.

And I saw it for the first time—not just the sigils carved into his chest, but the ones down his spine. Some inked. Some scarred. Some carved by his own hand, if the jaggedness of the lines meant anything.

I stopped a few steps away.

He didn't move.

Didn't acknowledge me.

But I could feel the way his breath changed.

He was trying to stay still.

Trying not to turn around.

Trying not to reach.

And I loved him for failing at it.

I came to him slowly.

Kneeling behind him, careful not to make a sound. Not out of fear.

Out of reverence.

He had made a vow in silence.

And now I would answer it the same way.

My hands found his shoulders.

Broad. Scarred. Warm.

He didn't flinch.

But I felt the breath punch out of him. Like I'd knocked something loose that had lived inside his ribs too long.

I leaned forward.

Pressed my lips to one of the sigils.

He inhaled sharply.

I kissed the next.

Then the next.

I moved down his back with my mouth, slowly, methodically, like I was reading him.

Like his skin was scripture.

And when I reached his lowest scar—just above the waistband of his robe—I pressed my cheek to it.

He whispered.

I almost didn't hear it.

"I never thought you'd want to see them."

"I need to," I said. "I need to know what kept you alive before I got here."

He turned then.

And I let him.

He faced me fully, the light from the windows catching his skin in a way that made the scars glow.

"You want to carry it," he said.

I nodded.

"I already do."

His mouth parted. His hands reached.

But they didn't grab.

They hovered. Framed my face.

"If I touch you now," he said, "it won't be to hollow."

"Then touch me like I'm already full."

He kissed me.

Not like a man starving.

Like a man who had already eaten and still wanted more.

He laid me down in front of the altar.

On the same stone where he once made me kneel.

But he didn't press me down.

He undressed me slowly. Not to expose. To reveal.

He let the fabric fall from my shoulders like ash, like memory. His hands moved in silence—lifting, peeling, tracing—not out of lust, but remembrance. Like he was reacquainting himself with the edges of something sacred. With the girl who hadn't flinched. The one who stayed.

He didn't rush.

He took his time with my body the way a priest might touch scripture—deliberate, slow, reverent. His fingers trailed over the line of my waist, the dip of my ribs, the curve of my hip. He cupped my ass in one palm and just... held it. As if cataloguing its weight. As if grounding himself in the proof that I was still there.

His other hand traced up my spine. Over my shoulder blades. Across the back of my neck. He didn't speak, didn't breathe heavy, didn't press forward yet. He just looked.

Looked at my skin like it remembered things he was afraid to forget.

When I turned to face him, his eyes found mine instantly. And he *saw* me. Every shiver. Every beat of want. Every place I had cracked to let him in.

His thumb brushed over my lower lip. Down to my collarbone. He followed it with his mouth—open, slow, warm. A kiss. A breath. A vow.

He guided me down with both hands. Careful. Unapologetically present. The stone was cold, but his body was not. He knelt between my legs and let them fall open like they'd been waiting.

He didn't spread me.

He watched me do it.

And then he touched me again.

Ran his fingers from the inside of my thigh to the crease of my hip. Palmed my stomach. Slid lower. Not seeking wetness. Not checking readiness.

Just *knowing* it.

When he pressed the head of his cock to me, he didn't thrust. He *watched* my face.

Waited.

And I met his eyes.

I let him see every part of me that had starved.

That had ached.

That had *stayed*.

And then he pushed.

Not fast.

Not deep.

Just *in*.

The stretch was tender, deliberate. He paused halfway, eyes still locked on mine, like he didn't want to miss the way it felt to be let in with permission. With trust. With want.

I gasped softly. And he exhaled.

Then moved deeper.

All the way.

Inside me like he was settling into something that had always been his.

His hand gripped my thigh.

His forehead met mine.

And he began to move.

Not to fuck.

To *remain*.

And when I came apart beneath him, trembling, gasping, whispering his name like a second vow—

He said mine in return.

And I heard it this time.

Not as claim.

But as confession.

And I kept it.

The ache didn't leave me after he fucked me. It changed.

It settled into something deeper. Not the sharp burn of being taken or the bruised throb of obedience. This was something else. Something quieter. Wider. It spread through my chest like breath I didn't remember learning to take.

He hadn't left. But he hadn't stayed curled around me either. He sat a few feet away, back pressed to the altar, robe loose at the shoulders, eyes closed like prayer but breathing like war.

I watched him through the dark, my hand resting on the place where he had just lived. My thighs still sticky with him. My body still open. Still his.

But he was further away now than he'd ever been.

And I couldn't bear it.

I crawled to him.

Not because I was afraid.

Because I needed to feel the shape of his body under my palms. I needed to remember that he wasn't myth. That he wasn't memory. That he was made of skin and blood and hunger like mine.

I reached for his hand.

He opened his eyes.

"Why are you looking at me like that?" I asked.

His voice was low.

"Because I don't know what to do with softness."

"You already did it."

He shook his head.

"That wasn't softness. That was need."

"What's the difference?"

He looked at me like I'd asked the only question that had ever mattered.

"Softness stays," he whispered. "Need eats."

I crawled into his lap. Straddled him. Took his face between my hands.

"Then stay."

His breath caught.

"I might not be able to want you gently."

"Then want me the way you need to."

He didn't move for a long time.

And then he kissed me.

And it wasn't gentle.

It was reverent.

He laid me back against the cold altar. Not the stone. Not the place we fucked. The real one. The high one. The one no one had dared climb since the Order left it to rot.

He laid me there like I was worthy of being sacrificed.

And then he undressed me again.

Not with urgency.

With awe.

He spread my legs and knelt between them. Bent his head and pressed his mouth to the inside of my thigh.

"Tell me," he said.

"What?" I breathed.

"Tell me who I am to you."

I shivered.

"You're not my god," I said.

"*No.*"

"You're not my savior."

"*No.*"

"*You're my altar.*"

He groaned. Bent lower. Licked me slow, like he wanted to swallow the truth of it. His mouth moved over my opening with steady reverence, tongue circling my clit until I shook. Until I gasped his name without shame.

He didn't rush.

He didn't speak.

He just devoured.

And when he fucked me again, it wasn't to break me.

It was to worship.

And I let him.

Because I knew now.

He wasn't here to erase me.

He was here to remember me.

To write my name in every breath he had left.

And I was already doing the same.

He bound my wrists with ribbon.

Not rope. Not chain. Not the stained silk they used to correct girls in the cloistered halls of the convent. This was soft. Pale. Unassuming. Like something meant to adorn rather than contain. But it held.

And I let it.

He didn't tie me because I needed to be silenced.

He tied me because I had asked to stay.

He wrapped the ribbon twice, then twice again, binding my hands together at the center of my chest like an offering made in breath. His fingers worked with a strange reverence, not looking at what he was doing, but at my mouth. Like he was waiting for it to part, to beg, to break.

It didn't.

I held the silence.

He adjusted the final knot. Tight. Secure. But not cruel.

Then he sat back on his heels, looked at me from where I lay on the robe, and said nothing.

And that nothing said everything.

I could feel the shift in him.

The heat wasn't gone. The hunger hadn't dulled. But something else had taken its place at the front of his mind.

Restraint.

Not for me.

For him.

He pulled my robe down, exposing me slowly. My breasts, my belly, the soft curve of my thighs. He didn't undress me like he was claiming something.

He did it like he was remembering.

Like he needed to see what he'd already written.

When his fingers ghosted over the tops of my thighs, I moaned.

Not because it was too much.

Because it was not enough.

"Tell me why you're quiet," he said.

I opened my eyes.

"Because I don't need to ask for what I know you'll give me."

He closed his eyes. Just for a second. Like the weight of that undid something in him.

When he moved over me, it was with precision. Not careful. Deliberate. Like he'd planned every inch. Like he'd waited for this.

His cock was hard. Heavy. He brushed it between my legs, not entering, just letting it rest against the place he'd already hollowed.

"Say it," he murmured.

"I'm yours."

"Say why you're bound."

"Because I stayed."

He pressed inside me in one, slow, devastating stroke.

I gasped. My back arched. My wrists pulled against the ribbon, not in protest, but in prayer. The pressure, the fullness, the unbearable rightness of being taken like this—without demand, without punishment. Just kept.

He fucked me clothed. His robes brushed against my thighs. His belt grazed my skin. There was something more obscene in it. More sacred. Like he hadn't bothered to become a man for this. Like he was still altar, still vow, still the dark thing I'd knelt before and asked to be unmade by.

His hand slid beneath my bound wrists.

Lifted them.

Held them above my head as he moved inside me with brutal grace.

He didn't speak again.

But I knew.

I felt it in every thrust.

In every pause.

In the way his breath stuttered against my mouth but never kissed it.

He was claiming me again.

Not with pain.

With permanence.

And when I came, it was a quiet thing.

A sob. A gasp. A silence.

And he followed with a groan so low I felt it more than heard it.

He collapsed into me. Not with weight. With trust.

He let go of my wrists. Untied them slowly. Let the ribbon fall away.

And I knew then:

It had never been about keeping me still.

It was about remembering that I chose to be.

And I would choose it again.

Every time.

I didn't expect him to let me hold him.

Not truly. Not in the way that mattered. I had touched him. Taken him. Worshipped him with my body, with my voice, with the ache between my legs. But this was different.

This was after.

The kind of after where breath doesn't come so easily. Where bodies remember they are still human, and silence becomes heavy with everything no one is willing to say.

He sat on the floor with his back to the altar, legs stretched, arms braced at his sides. His robes were still half on, the tie loosened but not removed, like he didn't know if he wanted to stay clothed or bare. Like even now, he was still deciding how much of himself he could survive being seen.

I knelt in front of him.

No ritual. No performance.

Just the quiet of knowing he had fucked me slowly, reverently, held my wrists in ribbon, whispered nothing, and still told me everything.

"Let me," I said.

He didn't ask what.

He didn't move.

But when I reached for his hand, he gave it to me.

Rough. Calloused. Strong in the way stone is strong.

I held it in both of mine. Brought it to my mouth.

Kissed each knuckle.

One by one.

Not like a girl who had been ruined.

Like a woman who remembered every bruise, and thanked him for it.

"You keep washing me," I said. "Let me wash you."

His breath caught.

Not loudly.

But I felt it. In his fingers. In the silence that followed.

He let me.

He let me bring the cloth and the basin and kneel beside him.

He let me remove what was left of his robe.

He let me see him—not the man who took, but the one who had once been told never to be touched again.

I wiped the sweat from his chest.

The blood from his lip where he'd bitten it while inside me.

The wax that had dried into the curve of his hip.

I pressed the cloth to the lines carved into his ribs.

He didn't flinch.

But I saw him shake.

"You always look like you're bracing to be hurt," I whispered.

He looked at me then.

And said nothing.

Because it was true.

I rinsed the cloth. Dipped it again. Brought it to his hands. Washed his fingers. His palms.

And then, slowly, I reached for his face.

He closed his eyes before I touched him.

But he didn't pull away.

And I knew what it meant.

I wiped the sweat from his temples. The smudge of ash from beneath his cheekbone. The shadow of something darker from the line of his throat.

When I was done, I set the cloth aside.

And he looked at me.

Like I had done something he would never forgive me for.

And would never stop being grateful for.

I pulled the blanket over his shoulders.

Wrapped it around both of us.

And let him rest his head against my chest.

He didn't speak.

He didn't breathe like a man who had claimed something.

He breathed like a man who had been kept.

And I kissed the crown of his head.

Because that's what he was now.

Not my vow.

Not my ruin.

Mine.

Chapter Ten

I woke before him.

For a long time, I didn't move.

His body was curled toward mine, one arm flung across my hips like possession even in sleep. His breath warmed the space between my shoulder blades, slow and steady. If I hadn't felt the weight of his hand or the rhythm of his chest behind me, I might have believed he was gone again.

But no.

He was here.

Still here.

And the stillness between us wasn't empty. It was something larger now. Something sacred. Something too vast to speak into.

I turned my head slightly, just enough to watch him without disturbing the fragile quiet we'd built.

His hair had come loose in the night, strands curling damply at his temple. His jaw was slack with sleep, mouth slightly parted. It made him look younger. Not softer. Just more real.

His chest bore the marks of my hands.

His neck, the faint echo of my teeth.

His hips, the bruises where I had gripped him when he fucked me with reverence.

I should have felt powerful.

But what I felt instead was claimed.

Because even now, with his eyes closed, with his body lax and his mind deep in whatever dreamless place he'd fled to, he didn't look like a man who had taken something.

He looked like a man who had finally been given something back.

Me.

I slid my hand to his wrist.

Held it.

Not tightly. Not like a chain.

Just enough to feel the pulse beneath my thumb. Just enough to prove to myself that he was still warm. Still alive.

His fingers curled reflexively. Not into a fist. Into mine.

I bit back the sound that rose in my throat.

It wasn't a sob.

It wasn't pleasure.

It was something heavier. Something born from the ache of having what I didn't think I could keep.

His hand flexed again, this time with intention. He pulled me tighter against him, his breath deepening. Still not awake. Still dreaming.

But it was me he reached for.

Me he sought even in sleep.

And that—that wrecked me more than any vow.

Because I knew now.

He wasn't keeping me.

He was holding on.

And I was the only thing left he hadn't let go of.

I pressed my mouth to the back of his hand.

Whispered his name like a benediction.

He stirred.

Didn't open his eyes.

But his voice broke through the hush like breath returning to a body.

"Still here?"

"Yes."

"Good."

His arm tightened around me.

"I didn't want to wake up without you."

And just like that, I wasn't afraid of the stillness anymore.

Because it wasn't the absence of movement.

It was the presence of us.

He asked me once what I wanted to be called.

Not the name they gave me. Not the one he whispered into my throat when I came on his cock. Not even the one written into the pages of the ledger that waited in silence for every girl to leave.

He asked with his eyes.

Lying on his side, shirtless, still sweat-slick from the vow we'd just made with breath and movement and the silence that followed. His hand cupped my hip like a relic. His gaze never dropped to my body.

Only my face.

"I don't know," I whispered. "What am I now?"

His jaw clenched. His thumb traced the hollow beneath my ribs. He looked at me like I had asked him to carve scripture with his teeth.

"You're the place I remember I'm still alive," he said.

And then he didn't speak for hours.

We sat together by the edge of the basin. The water hadn't been changed. He didn't ask me to kneel. I didn't offer. There was nothing to prove.

Not anymore.

He watched me as I bathed myself.

Washed his come from my thighs. My neck. The places where his hands had marked me. He didn't look away.

And I didn't cover myself.

Because what was there to hide, now?

He'd fucked me until I couldn't remember my own voice.

Then kissed me like it was the only thing he knew how to hear.

I dipped a cloth into the water and turned to him.

"Your turn."

He said nothing.

But he let me come to him.

I pressed the cloth to his chest.

Over the sigils. The scars. The places I'd kissed but never named.

He held still. His breath sharp. His body tense.

But he didn't stop me.

When I was done, I sat beside him again. Shoulder to shoulder. Bare skin against scar.

"You were never supposed to be soft," I said.

"And now?"

I looked at him.

"Now I know softness is what happens when discipline falls in love with surrender."

He didn't speak.

But his hand found mine.

And that was answer enough.

Later, when the chapel darkened again and the fire curled in the hearth like a secret, he touched me beneath the robe I wore.

Not to claim.

To remember.

His fingers traced my ribs. The curve of my breast. The inside of my thigh. No urgency. Just knowing.

And I realized then—

He had hollowed me.

But now he was learning to live inside what he'd made.

And I was letting him.

Because if I had become sanctuary,

Then he had become the prayer I no longer needed to speak.

I needed to see him undone.

Not ruined. Not broken. I'd seen him fierce, still, cruel in silence and savage in worship. I'd felt the weight of his body claiming mine like a vow written in skin. But I had not seen him surrender.

Not the kind that bled. The kind that asked to be held.

He was always composed. Measured. Like control was the only thing that kept his hunger from swallowing him whole.

But I didn't want his control anymore.

I wanted his ache.

I found him by the altar.

Not kneeling.

Sitting. Legs stretched out, robes loosened at his waist, hair falling around his face in dark, tangled waves. His hands were braced on either side of him like he didn't trust his body not to move on its own.

His eyes tracked me before his head turned.

Not like a predator.

Like a man who couldn't believe he was still being chosen.

I crossed the space between us slowly.

Each step louder than it should have been. Not because the stone echoed. Because he watched each one like a confession.

I didn't ask.

I straddled him.

The robe fell open around my hips, bare beneath. My knees found the outside of his thighs. My pussy pressed against the hardness he tried not to name.

His hands hovered.

"You don't have to," he said.

I reached for the collar of his robe.

Pulled it from his shoulders.

"Yes," I said. "I do."

I laid him down.

Slow. Reverent. The way he had laid me down so many times before. His body stiffened beneath me, not from resistance, but memory. His back arched as my hands moved over his chest.

He didn't stop me.

Even when I pressed my mouth to the mark above his heart.

Even when I whispered,

"Let me take you."

He turned his face away.

But he let me pull the robe from his hips.

His cock was hard. Already. Waiting.

I wrapped my hand around it. Felt the pulse beneath my palm.

He hissed through his teeth.

"Breathe," I said.

He did.

And I took him into my mouth.

Slowly.

The way he'd taken me.

Not to tease.

To remember.

He groaned. His fingers twisted into the robe beneath him. His thighs tensed. But he didn't guide me. Didn't thrust.

He let me choose how to worship.

When I climbed back up his body, I didn't ask.

I sank down on his cock like it was the only answer left in the world.

He gasped.

"Let me," I whispered.

His eyes locked on mine.

And he let me fuck him.

I rode him until his head fell back, until his voice broke open, until the walls of the chapel could no longer hold the sound of him saying my name.

And when he came, he held me like he didn't know what to do with the tenderness.

And I kept him there.

Because he needed to learn.

That surrender didn't mean weakness.

It meant want.

And I wanted him more than I wanted breath.

Because he was not my god.

He was my altar.

And tonight, I was the offering.

I didn't tell him where I was going.

I didn't have to. He watched me cross the chapel like a prayer he didn't dare interrupt. I wasn't quiet. I wasn't slow. I didn't perform for him. I just walked.

Naked under the robe, my skin still wore the marks of him—teeth, bruise, sweat-dried salt. The ache in my thighs was dull now, threaded through with memory. Not pain. Not need. Presence.

I passed the altar.

The basin.

The stone that had once held me like a punishment.

And I went to the far wall.

There, etched into the stone, were names. Dozens. Hundreds. Some so old the letters had faded into dust. Others deeper, darker. Some scratched out. Some underlined.

A ledger carved not on pages.

On walls.

I didn't look for mine.

I didn't look for hers.

I didn't touch the names.

I touched the space between them.

The empty stone.

And I pressed my palm flat.

And I moaned his name.

Low. Slow. Thick with the tremble that started at the base of my spine and coiled through me like reverence.

Not loud enough to echo.

But enough to feel it leave me.

Enough to feel it stay.

I sank to my knees.

I touched myself.

One hand between my legs, the other still pressed to the wall like an invocation. My fingers moved slow. Not to come. *To remember*.

The way he fucked me. The way he touched me when he didn't mean to. The way his voice faltered when he called me his like the word was too sacred to hold.

I moved in rhythm with the memory of him.

With the rhythm he carved into me with his hips. With his vow. With the stillness he left behind.

I didn't close my eyes.

Because I knew he was watching.

I felt his gaze burn across my spine, down my arms, over the stretch of my thighs. I knew he wouldn't interrupt.

Because this was worship.

And he understood it now.

When I came, I said nothing.

Only his name.

And when I opened my eyes, he was there.

Across the chapel.

Kneeling.

Head bowed.

Not like a man in prayer.

Like a man undone.

And I knew then:

This chapel wasn't mine.

He was.

And I was the only name he would never carve into the wall.

Because I was the space he filled.

And that was enough.

He bound me again that night.

Not for silence. Not for stillness. Not for obedience. I didn't need help remembering how to stay.

He did it because I asked.

Not with words. With the way I lay down.

The way I folded my hands across my chest like prayer.

The way I looked at him and didn't flinch when he pulled the ribbon from the basin where it soaked in warm water and sacred memory.

He knelt beside me, bare to the waist, hair tied at the base of his neck with a leather strip. His breath was even. His movements reverent. But his eyes were wrecked. Starved. Wide with the weight of what he hadn't said.

He didn't ask if I was sure.

He never did.

He wrapped the ribbon once. Twice. Around my wrists, crossed and resting over my heart. He didn't pull tight. He didn't knot it like a threat. He let it rest like breath against breath.

He looked at me then.

"You were never mine," he said.

I didn't answer.

I didn't have to.

Because I was still there.

He lowered himself beside me.

Not touching.

Not reaching.

Just close.

And I felt it—that sacred ache. The one that doesn't come from need. The one that comes after. The one that says: we are still here.

He lay on his side, one hand beneath his head, the other resting against the stone between us. His fingertips brushed the edge of the robe.

Not my skin.

But near.

I stared at the ceiling.

It was cracked. Broken in places where the weight of time had pulled it inward.

But it held.

Just like us.

He didn't speak again. Not that night.

But his presence said everything.

That I wasn't meant to be corrected.

That he wasn't meant to be forgiven.

That we weren't meant to be saved.

We were meant to be kept.

When I finally slept, I dreamed of his hands.

Not binding.

Holding.

Not punishing.

Keeping.

And when I woke, the ribbon was still there.

My wrists still bound.

My body still marked.

And him?

He was watching me.

Not like a priest.

Not like a keeper.

Like a man who had vowed himself to a single altar.

And knew he would never kneel at another.

Chapter Eleven

I asked him to bind me again.

Not because I needed to be controlled.

Because I needed him to remember what he had made—what he had built inside me with nothing but fire and silence.

The first time he tied my wrists, it was obedience.

The second was a ritual.

But this time—it was mine.

This was not stillness. Not submission. This was the sanctity of being *witnessed.*

I stood before him, naked beneath the robe I hadn't bothered to tie. My hands were already lifted, wrists crossed over my chest, palms angled like a vow I was offering him without shame. Like relic. Like proof.

He sat on the edge of the altar like a man who had forgotten how to pray.

He didn't speak.

He rose.

Moved toward me.

His robe dragged behind him like sin worn thin from worship.

And when he reached into the basin and drew out the soaked ribbon, I realized—he had waited for this. Hoped for it.

He stepped behind me, and his heat touched my back before his hands did.

I didn't turn.

I closed my eyes.

And waited.

His fingers brushed my skin, not hurried, not hesitant—just certain. The silk whispered around my wrists like breath. He wrapped slowly, reverently, like a priest preparing an offering. Not to bind. To anoint.

He didn't knot.

He didn't pull tight.

He held.

And then he lowered his head.

His mouth met the inside of my wrists—once, twice—soft and slow. Not like a man claiming what he owned.

But like a man kissing something he didn't believe he deserved.

I trembled.

Not from fear.

From ache.

From the unbearable weight of being wanted like this.

He turned me gently.

Faced me.

Looked down at what he had tied—what I had offered—and breathed like it hurt to see me still there.

"Do you know what you are now?" he asked, voice like coal scraped through velvet.

"Yes," I said.

"Say it."

"I'm yours."

His eyes flickered like flame.

"But not because I made you."

"No," I whispered. "Because I wanted to be."

That truth hit him like scripture. He inhaled sharply, like it branded him from the inside.

Then he stepped back.

Sat.

Spread his knees.

Held out a hand.

"Come kneel."

I did.

Not because I was told.

Because I wanted to be seen the way he saw me—holy.

I walked slowly.

Let the robe fall.

Let the cold kiss my skin.

And then I dropped to my knees between his legs.

Bound.

Bare.

Burning.

He didn't touch me.

He just *watched.*

And somehow that undid me more than anything else ever could.

He didn't spread his arms.

Didn't reach for his cock.

He sat like a vow—still, silent, waiting.

My knees ached.

But I stayed.

Because this wasn't submission.

This was *worship.*

"Do you know what you are now?" he asked again.

"Yes," I breathed.

He drank me in with his gaze.

And I let him.

"Tell me."

"I am the place you return to."

His breath caught.

"Say it again."

"I am where you come back."

He shifted.

I saw his cock harden beneath the fabric of his robe.

He didn't free it.

He didn't move.

He *endured* the want.

"You want to be kept?" he asked.

"I already am."

His hand flexed against the stone.

I tilted my head.

"Then keep me too," I said.

He groaned.

A low, broken sound like a prayer that had been denied too long.

Still—he didn't reach.

So I did.

Bound, bare, trembling—I leaned in.

I pressed my mouth to his thigh. Then higher.

His cock twitched beneath his robe.

I wanted to feel it.

I wanted to take it.

"Let me show you what it means to be kept."

And I did.

I undressed him like I was stripping away history.

The robe fell like ash from his shoulders. Heavy with memory. With myth.

He let me.

That was the vow.

He let me see all of him.

The scars. The shadows. The weight he carried in silence.

I climbed into his lap.

Straddled him.

My bound hands brushed his chest. His breath faltered.

My pussy throbbed, slick and swollen, aching for him.

I ground against him, and he gasped.

I reached between us, undid his belt.

Pulled the fabric down his hips.

His cock sprang free, thick and hot, flushed with want.

Still, he didn't guide me.

He just watched.

"You want to?"

"No," I said. "I *need* to."

I sank down on him in one long, slow slide.

His mouth opened.

No sound came out.

Because I had taken it from him.

I rode him slow. Reverent. My wrists bound. My mouth parted.

He watched me like he was watching scripture unfold.

I fucked him like I was claiming every vow he never spoke.

His head fell back.

His hands gripped the edge of the altar.

And when he came, it wasn't a roar.

It was a *prayer*.

I followed.

Trembling. *Wrecked.*

And he caught me.

Because he knew.

He had hollowed me.

And now—I had filled him.

Chapter Twelve

He fed me that morning.

Not with worship.

Not with command.

Just with his hands.

Quiet. Steady. Still half-cloaked in the silence that wrapped itself around us like old cloth.

He laid the food out on a piece of linen—a wedge of cheese, a cut of bread, and two pieces of fruit.

One red. One gold.

I sat across from him in the low light near the altar. My thighs still trembled from where he had filled me. My wrists still carried the mark of the ribbon he had used to bind me. My body ached like it had been sanctified and cracked open and made new.

He passed me the gold fruit.

His fingers brushed mine.

That was all.

No ceremony.

Just care.

I brought it to my mouth.

Bit into the skin.

Sweetness burst on my tongue. Ripe. Soft. Familiar.

But then—

The taste shifted.

There was a sourness under the surface. A softness that wasn't meant to be there.

I pulled the fruit away. Turned it in my hand.

The other side was bruised.

Not black. Not ruined.

But wrong.

Browning.

Spoiled from the inside out.

Sweetness sliding into rot.

I chewed anyway.

I swallowed.

And the aftertaste clung to my throat like grief.

He didn't speak.

Or he noticed—and chose not to.

That was worse.

I set the fruit down. Wiped my fingers on my thigh.

And suddenly the chapel felt smaller.

Not sacred.

Suffocating.

The fire had grown cold. The basin was dry. The robe he'd worn still lay across the altar, neatly folded like a ritual left unfinished.

The silence didn't soothe me.

It scraped.

"Is this all there is?" I asked.

His head turned.

"Here?" he said.

I nodded.

He didn't answer.

And that silence said more than any yes ever could.

I looked down at the food, the clean linen, the soft ache in my belly. And I realized—

This was stillness, not life.

This was memory on repeat.

This was the moment *after* the vow, when nothing moves and everything starts to ruin.

Even worship spoils if left untouched.

I stood.

He didn't follow.

He just watched.

"I need... to know what else there is," I said.

He didn't speak.

But something in his jaw tightened.

Like I'd struck a sacred chord.

He walked to me.

Lifted the ribbon from the table.

He didn't bind me.

He didn't ask me to stay.

He handed it to me.

"In case you forget what your hands are for," he said.

My throat closed.

I reached for him.

He kissed my fingers.

And let go.

I walked to the chapel doors.

My robe loose around my shoulders. The ribbon clutched in my hand like a relic.

And I stepped outside.

Not because I wanted freedom.

But because I wanted hunger.

Because I needed to remember what starving for him felt like.

The air outside didn't feel like air.

It felt like absence.

Like breath I hadn't earned. Like light that had never touched me before.

The sky was pale and too open. The wind had no weight.

I blinked against the brightness.

And I felt my ribs curl inward.

Because everything out here moved.

And nothing here saw me.

I walked.

Not fast. Not with purpose.

Just forward.

The ground was soft. The soil forgiving. Grass touched my feet like apology.

But none of it felt holy.

It felt indifferent.

I pressed the ribbon into my palm.

Tight.

Until I could pretend it was still his hand.

The sun touched my skin.

The robe clung to my legs.

But I didn't stop.

I walked until the light changed.

Until the ache in my feet matched the ache in my chest.

Until I found a house.

Small. Wooden. Human.

A woman opened the door.

She didn't ask questions.

She fed me.

Let me bathe.

And when she touched my wrist—

Gently, kindly, sweetly—

I flinched.

Because it wasn't rough enough to mean anything.

Because she didn't tremble.

Because kindness without need is not devotion. It's distance.

That night, I stared at the ceiling.

And realized stillness here was not sacred.

It was silence with no vow.

I clutched the ribbon.

Held it to my chest.

And wept.

Not from grief.

From hunger.

Because no amount of soup could feed what he had carved into me.

Because I didn't want peace.

I wanted to ache for something again.

I whispered his name.

Once.

Twice.

Until the air remembered how it sounded.

And then I knew.

I hadn't left to escape.

I had left to starve.

And now I was starving.

Chapter Thirteen

THE SUN WAS TOO SOFT.

It filtered through the window like warm breath, touching the bed where I lay with the kind of light that was supposed to feel comforting.

It didn't.

It felt like trespass.

Like light that didn't know me. That hadn't watched me bleed on stone or kneel for something bigger than mercy. It felt foreign, like it had never seen a girl wrecked by a vow, had never heard a name moaned into sacred silence.

The sheets beneath me were linen. Clean. Smelling faintly of lavender and earth and everything I had once been told a girl should want. But my body ached for cold. For stone. For the scratch of wool against bruises and the weight of his breath against my spine.

I rolled onto my side. The movement felt wrong.

My legs didn't protest.

My thighs didn't burn.

My core didn't pulse from being full.

And that emptiness felt worse than pain.

I pressed my face into the pillow and inhaled.

It smelled like dust.

Like air that had never held his silence.

I stayed there a long time.

Not crying.

Not sleeping.

Just trying to remember what it felt like to belong to someone who knew how to hold my ruin like it was sacred.

The woman who took me in said nothing when I didn't come to breakfast.

She knocked once.

Left a bowl of soup.

A piece of bread.

A ribbon tied loosely around the edge of a folded note with nothing written inside.

Not red.

Not stained.

Just clean.

That was the part that broke me.

I untied it and set it on the floor like it burned.

Then I drank the soup.

It was warm.

But not sacred.

It didn't taste like silence soaked in restraint.

It didn't carry the weight of his breath.

It filled my stomach.

But not the ache.

I chewed the bread slowly. It was soft in the center. Crisp at the edges. The kind of food that means survival.

But I didn't want survival.

I wanted something brutal.

Something holy.

Something that left a mark.

I stared out the window for a long time after that.

The grass moved in soft waves.

The sky bled blue and gold.

Birds called each other by names I no longer remembered.

And all of it felt like a world that belonged to someone else.

Because the only thing I remembered was him.

His hands. His mouth. The way he looked at me when I said *don't stop*. The way he pressed my wrists together like they were scripture. The way his silence bent time.

The way I left him kneeling, and he didn't rise.

I pressed my hand to my chest.

Felt the hollow shape where his name used to sit.

It wasn't grief.

It was starvation.

Of a different kind.

The kind that lived in the wrists.

In the hips.

In the place behind the ribs where breath turns into prayer.

And I hated it.

Because I was full of air.

And none of it tasted like him.

I curled around the ache.

Not to sleep.

To remember.

Because the last time I was truly still—he was the weight beside me.

And now I was weightless.

And it was unbearable.

The mirror in the room was small.

Cracked.

Nailed to the wall like an afterthought.

I stared too long.

The reflection looked like me.

But it didn't *feel* like me.

This version of me had soft skin and clean hair and steady breath.

But no bruises.

No scripture.

No bite marks shaped like belonging.

This wasn't the girl who had bled on stone and been called sacred for it.

This was someone new.

Someone gentled.

Someone *lost*.

I pulled the shirt over my head.

Let it fall to the floor.

I stood naked in the middle of the room, waiting to feel something.

I pressed my fingers to my breasts.

To the inside of my wrists.

To the place between my thighs.

Nothing.

No shiver.

No ache.

No heat.

And that scared me more than anything.

Because it meant I was already forgetting what it felt like to be his.

I bathed in the basin. The water was scented with lavender and rosemary.

It made me want to cry.

Because he had never used perfume.

Only silence.

Only fire.

Only the cloth he wrung with purpose.

And it had been enough.

I dressed again. Slowly.

Every stitch of fabric a betrayal.

The clothes were too soft.

Nothing clung. Nothing scratched.

Nothing reminded me of the weight I used to carry.

I walked outside.

Let my feet touch earth.

It didn't hurt.

And I hated that.

Because pain was proof.

And this—

This was forgetting.

I stood in the sun until my skin itched.

I watched a woman hang laundry. Her skirt danced in the wind.

She didn't see me.

No one did.

And maybe that was worse than being rejected.

Because in that chapel, every gasp was holy.

Every moan, memorized.

Every bruise, remembered.

But here?

Here, I was just a girl with a quiet mouth and no vow to hold it open.

I touched the place between my legs.

Found only absence.

Closed my eyes.

Whispered his name.

The wind didn't carry it.

Because he wasn't here to hear it.

And the silence?

It wasn't sacred anymore.

It was *empty*.

I forgot what day it was.

Not because I lost track.

Because time had stopped mattering the moment I left his hands.

I touched the ribbon more often than I meant to.

I slept with it beneath my pillow.

Folded across my chest like a prayer that refused to die.

I didn't speak his name aloud.

Because it tasted too much like a vow I had broken.

The woman left food.

She warmed water.

She was kind.

But kindness isn't the same as being *kept*.

And I had been kept.

I stopped eating.

Not to punish myself.

Because the fruit had no bruise.

The bread had no salt.

The soup had no silence in it.

And I missed the ache.

I missed the way he tied my wrists.

The way he watched me breathe like it meant something.

The way he worshipped me in stillness.

The way he wrecked me with reverence.

One night, I tried to sleep again in that bed.

I woke with my hand between my legs.

His name on my tongue.

I came.

Quietly.

And I cried.

Because he wasn't there to hold it.

Because he wasn't watching.

Because I had left.

And he had let me.

I stood at the door the next morning.

Ribbon in hand.

Barefoot.

And ready.

Not for forgiveness.

Not for rescue.

But for ruin.

Because I was done pretending I could be whole without the hands that had hollowed me.

I walked.

Back toward the stone.

Back toward the man who tied silence into my skin like scripture.

Because he was the only vow I had ever meant.

And I needed to be ruined by him again.

Chapter Fourteen

He looked smaller when I returned.

Not diminished. Not broken.

Just—hollowed.

Like the shape of him had stayed, but the man inside had been scraped thinner by every breath I didn't take beside him.

The chapel hadn't changed.

The stone still bled cold into the soles of my feet.

The altar still loomed like it had never been touched, though we'd both bled on it.

But he—

He had unraveled in silence.

His hair was looser than I'd ever seen it, falling over his shoulders in thick, tangled strands. The color dulled at the ends, like he hadn't touched water since I left. His cheeks were sharper. The hollows beneath his eyes darker. His mouth, cracked.

He looked like someone who had forgotten what it meant to be touched.

I wanted to reach for him.

But I waited.

Because this ache—this ruin—I needed to see it first. I needed to witness what my absence had carved.

He knelt at the base of the altar.

Not like a man repenting.

Like a man who didn't remember how to rise.

The firepit was cold.

The basin dry.

The candle wax on the floor had hardened into pale streaks, like rivers turned to bone.

Dust covered the edge of the altar.

His robe hung limp around his frame.

His wrists were bare. No ribbon. No blade.

He hadn't moved.

Not to tend.

Not to pray.

Not even to survive.

I stood in the doorway and watched him breathe.

Shallow.

Controlled.

But not strong.

Like the ritual of it had become habit without meaning.

Like he had stayed alive, but not living.

He hadn't eaten.

He hadn't slept.

He had waited.

Not for rescue.

Not for salvation.

For me.

Because I had hollowed him, too.

He turned his head slowly.

The sound of my breath cracked through the chapel like a breaking vow.

His eyes met mine.

And everything fell apart inside me.

The ache.

The hunger.

The way his gaze reached into me like a hand that had never stopped reaching.

"You came back," he said.

His voice was ruined.

Not from sadness.

From disuse.

It scraped out of him like something that didn't belong to air. Like a blade pulled from old stone.

"Yes," I whispered.

My voice didn't echo.

It landed.

Right between us.

Heavy.

True.

He didn't move.

But his silence did.

It wrapped around me.

Pulled.

Held.

Like arms he no longer trusted himself to raise.

I stepped forward.

One step.

Two.

Three.

Until I was close enough to feel the space where we used to breathe each other.

He didn't look at me.

He looked at my feet.

And I understood.

It wasn't that I had come back.

It was that he didn't believe I would kneel.

So I did.

Not because I owed him.

Not because he asked.

Because I wanted him to see me choose it.

Because this—this silence—was mine too.

My knees hit stone.

And his breath hitched.

A sharp, unholy sound. Like something sacred splitting in half.

His hand lifted.

Not to possess.

To steady.

And I let him.

Because this wasn't surrender.

It was return.

It was home.

We didn't speak.

We didn't need to.

Our bodies stayed still. Our knees nearly touched. Our breath threaded between us like something frayed and fragile and unbearably alive.

He had emptied himself in the time I was gone.

I could see it.

He sat like a vessel someone had forgotten to refill.

His palms faced the ceiling. Offering nothing.

Everything.

I reached for the ribbon.

The one he gave me when I left.

The one I had bled on in the dark.

It was frayed now. Stained. A knot I couldn't untie.

I held it out.

Hands shaking.

Not from fear.

From reverence.

From ache.

From the unbearable tenderness of being witnessed.

He didn't take it.

His mouth opened.

And then—

A whisper. Low. Cracked. Unbearably soft.

"I thought I hollowed you."

My throat closed.

"You did."

His voice broke again.

"But it's your name that echoes in my bones."

The ribbon slipped from my fingers.

I let it fall.

Because we didn't need it anymore.

Because we were already written.

I rose to my knees.

Lifted my hand.

Placed it on his chest.

Right over the place I had kissed once and called sacred.

His breath stopped.

Not held.

Given.

"You've been inside me since the fire," I whispered.

"And I never left you."

His eyes closed.

A tear slipped down.

He didn't wipe it away.

And I didn't name it.

Because this wasn't confession.

It was recognition.

It was the vow without ritual.

The prayer without words.

The keeping without chains.

He opened his eyes.

And said:

"Then hollow me again. And this time... don't let me leave."

He didn't beg.

He vowed.

And it broke me.

Because I had waited to hear those words since the moment I knelt in his silence the first time.

I crawled into his lap.

Slow. Like I was moving through sacred time.

He didn't reach for me.

He waited.

And I touched him like I was writing a new scripture.

I unfastened his robe.

Pushed it back.

Pressed my lips to the center of his chest.

Right over the sigil.

He groaned.

A sound torn from reverence.

Not lust.

Need.

I straddled him.

Took him in my hand.

Watched his mouth part.

Watched his head fall back.

And whispered—

"You're mine now."

And then I sank down onto him.

Not to fuck.

To reclaim.

To make a space inside me for him to live.

His hands gripped my hips like he didn't trust he was real.

I moved slowly.

With worship.

With ache.

With devotion so deep I could feel the chapel tilt.

He pressed his face to my throat.

Bit my skin like it would keep him from weeping.

I rode him until he broke.

Until I broke.

Until we weren't two bodies anymore.

Just vow.

Just echo.

Just us.

When he came, he didn't groan.

He exhaled.

Like a man finally emptied.

And I stayed there.

Full of him.

Marked.

Made.

Ours.

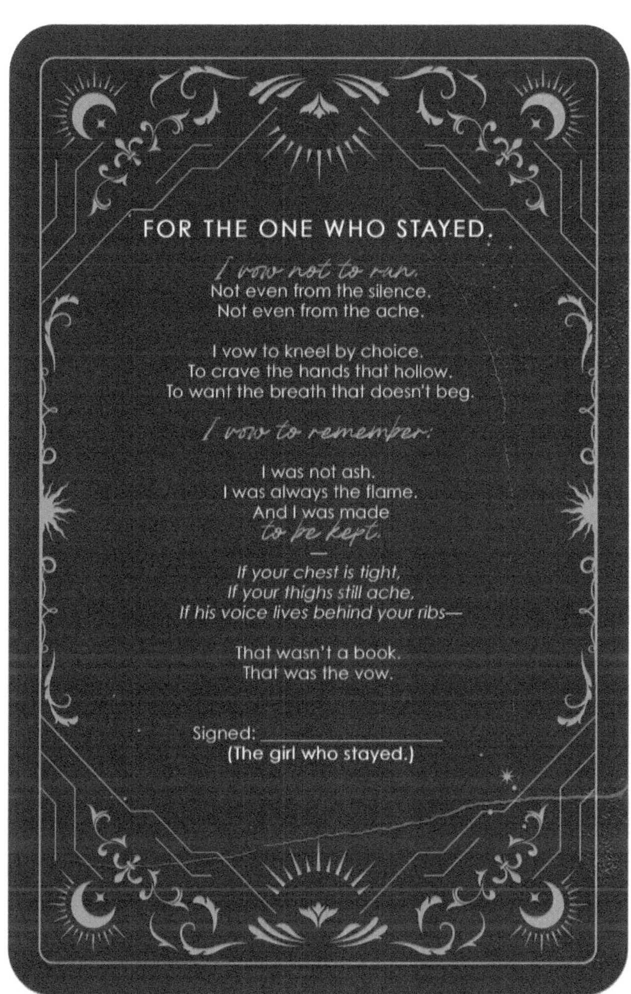

FOR THE ONE WHO STAYED.

I vow not to run.
Not even from the silence.
Not even from the ache.

I vow to kneel by choice.
To crave the hands that hollow.
To want the breath that doesn't beg.

I vow to remember:

I was not ash.
I was always the flame.
And I was made
to be kept.
—
If your chest is tight,
If your thighs still ache,
If his voice lives behind your ribs—

That wasn't a book.
That was the vow.

Signed: _______________
(The girl who stayed.)

You stayed.
You bled.
You burned.
And you were not erased.
If your chest is tight,
If your throat aches,
If something in you feels changed—
That was the vow.
You weren't made to be saved.
You were made to be *kept*.

Close the book when you're ready.
Not because it's over—
but because the silence deserves to stay.
This isn't the end.
It's just the first time someone saw you.

When you're ready for the next descent...
I'll be waiting at the altar.
—A.K. Rose

www.ingramcontent.com/pod-product-compliance
Lightning Source LLC
Chambersburg PA
CBHW032010180726
48283CB00008B/2617